HARMONICA'S BRIDEGROOM

PAUL BINDING (b. 1943) is a novelist, critic, poet and cultural historian. After spending his early childhood in Germany, he returned to be educated in England and studied English Literature at Oxford. He has been a lecturer at universities in Sweden, Mississippi, and Italy and was a managing editor for Oxford University Press and an editor for the *New Statesman*. His first novel, *Harmonica's Bridegroom* (1984), was well reviewed by critics and earned accolades from novelists James Purdy and Brian Moore. Other novels have included *Kingfisher Weather* (1989); *My Cousin the Writer* (2006), chosen as book of the year by Francis King and deemed a 'masterpiece' by the *Spectator*; and, most recently, the critically acclaimed *After Brock* (2012).

Besides his novels, Binding frequently contributes reviews to *The Independent*, *The Times Literary Supplement*, and others, and is the author of several non-fiction works, including *Lorca: The Gay Imagination* (1985), *St. Martin's Ride* (1990) (a memoir), *Eudora Welty: Portrait of a Writer* (1994), and a study of the artist in Ibsen (2006).

For more than twenty years, Binding has been involved with the promotion of Scandinavian literature and culture. His latest work, *Hans Christian Andersen: European Witness*, is forthcoming from Yale University Press in April 2014. He lives in Shropshire.

PAUL BINDING

Harmonica's Bridegroom

WITH A NEW AFTERWORD BY THE AUTHOR

VALANCOURT BOOKS

Harmonica's Bridegroom by Paul Binding
First published Henley-on-Thames: Aidan Ellis, 1984
First Valancourt Books edition 2014
Reprinted from the 1985 Black Swan edition

Published by Valancourt Books, Richmond, Virginia
Publisher & Editor: James D. Jenkins
20th Century Series Editor: Simon Stern, University of Toronto
http://www.valancourtbooks.com

978-1-939140-95-1 (*trade paperback*)
Also available as an electronic book.

All Valancourt Books publications are printed on acid free paper
that meets all ANSI standards for archival quality paper.

Cover by M. S. Corley
Set in Dante MT 11/13.2

Part One

I

Eleven o'clock at night, and somebody, somewhere on the broad tree-lined promenade of the Paseo de Recoletos, was playing a harmonica. His tune Daniel Varney recognised immediately as 'Wildwood Flower'; it had been a favourite of another harmonica player, his own brother, James. It should, Dan thought, be emanating now from the porch of some white wooden house in the American South, proceeding through a darkness fragrant with honeysuckle, punctuated by lightning bugs. Its yearning strains were surprising on Madrid's main avenue on the eve of the sixth anniversary of General Franco's death, and at a time when he was highly vulnerable to any reminders of his younger brother.

Already the young Franquistas, impatient for the demonstrations of the next day, were vaunting themselves in the roadway, in flag-decked cars which they drove at arrogant, intolerant speeds. In gleeful collusion they rhythmically honked horns, exchanged salutes, cried out '*España!*' to city and sky. And against all this an invisible musician went on with a wordless song of tender passion in secret woods.

Eventually Dan came upon him – alone on one of the walk's recessed benches, framed by lamplit plane-trees. He did not, it had to be admitted, much resemble James. He was wearing the tell-tale red sweater and red socks, and was sitting with his legs wide apart. So, Dan said to himself, at once sorry and pleased, this maker of music that challenges Fascist brouhaha and which reminds me of a loved brother standing with cupped hands in an Oxfordshire garden is no different from any other youth out on the promenade at this hour. His harmonica is only an unusual means of attracting cruising men.

Such as myself! . . . Dan positioned himself before the bench. The boy was slim, dark and neatly dressed, and he gave Dan a

5

darting look in which appraisal and enticement were equally combined. Then, casting his gaze back down upon the mauve and cream marble of the pavement, he continued his tune to its end, which he celebrated with three vibrant chords . . . Sometimes, after particularly good renderings of a tune – of 'Sugar in the Gourd', 'Down Yonder' or 'Done Gone' – Dan would beg James for repeats, requests that had almost always been granted. Dan felt inclined to ask this youth now – who played so strangely like that other of years ago – for a repetition of his air. But he didn't. Instead, he said in stiff, uneasy Spanish: 'Very good! You certainly know how to play the harmonica.' Then he added, hearing the anxious hope in his voice: 'Do you understand *any* English?'

The youth let the gaze of his near-black eyes rest upon Dan's face. 'Should understand it,' he said softly, 'it's my own bloody language after all.'

No young Spaniard's guttural whisper, but the overfamiliar accent of southern England's middle class. Looking at him more closely, Dan wondered how even a brief inspection could have led him to suppose the musician Spanish. His curly, cropped hair might be a glistening black, but his complexion was a pink-and-white English one. Nor, he now realised, was he exactly a youth. He was, Dan reckoned, about twenty-four.

'Is it so much of a shock – finding out that someone who's caught your eye is the same nationality as yourself?' he was being asked. The young man had taken from his left-hand pocket a handkerchief, also red, with which he was now carefully wiping the harmonica. The instrument was an old model, resembling one that James himself had once proudly owned – with many stops, and with gothic lettering embossed on its upper surface.

'Not a shock, no,' Dan replied, 'just something that I hadn't anticipated.'

'So now all those little compliments and icebreakers that you've been rehearsing for some Spanish boy have turned out useless,' this young compatriot observed with a truculent grin. 'And that, speaking from previous experience, takes quite a bit of getting over. You feel cheated.'

'I feel relieved,' said Dan, 'my Spanish isn't up to much.'

'It certainly isn't,' said the young man. 'But what about the English dread?'

'English dread?'

'Of meeting someone from their own fucking goldfish bowl of a country. A dread that before so very long there'll take place a conversation that'll go something like this,' and here he assumed a strangulatedly hoity-toity voice, ' "You don't by any chance know X, do you? I wonder if you've ever come across Y in your travels?" '

His eyes are like sloes sprinkled with rain, Dan thought appreciatively. But what a bitter expression they've got.

And bitter too was the tone of his next remarks. 'I'll bet you anything you like that I can read your thoughts: "Now what kind of background does this pretty-boy come from? Not one that usually produces a trader on the Recoletos, I'll be bound. There must be something funny somewhere." '

'Well, maybe you're not so very far off the mark,' Dan said, 'though I wouldn't have put it all so unsympathetically.' To himself he said; *my* background and *my* present activity might constitute a juxtaposition every bit as surprising.

Just then a shouted slogan broke into these reflections like the crack of a whip: '¡MUERTE A LA DEMOCRACIA!' Everything seemed to quiver at these words: the tall, grandiose buildings that lined the Paseo, the lamplit trees, the lamps that stood like metal herons. A handsome young couple in a gleaming sportscar passed by the recess, repeating the vile words with evident elation.

'Stupid bastards,' the harmonica-player muttered. Then, more loudly and, to Dan: 'What does it feel like to *be* them, I wonder. Perhaps best not to know. *They* probably wonder what it feels like to be *me* – loitering with intent on a gay promenade with a mouth-organ at my lips. Anyway,' and he gave Dan a quizzical glance, 'we should be grateful to them, don't you think?'

'Grateful!' exclaimed Dan, astonished, and shouting against the cacophony of horns that followed the slogans, 'why on earth should we be grateful?'

How could this young man have guessed the troubling, private significance these demonstrations, these articulated sentiments had for him? I should have grown out of this vicarious guilt years ago, Dan admonished himself. But then so much growing up that one expected to do one never achieved.

'Because they make us understand things.'

'What things?'

'Oh, life,' said the boy with an insolent airiness, 'what this whole stinking world of ours is all about. It isn't just made up of nice boys making pretty music on park benches, you know. Or of kindly older men speaking to them courteously.'

Older men, repeated Dan, to himself, a little nettled. I'm only thirty-eight. But the young man was trying both to shock and to provoke him – that was unmistakeable. All this self-conscious misanthropy. And, Dan asked himself, having embarked on this odd, unexpected conversation, what do I do now? Wouldn't it be best to move on? He was, in fact, pretty tired, having arrived in Madrid only late yesterday night (Friday); Monday morning was an important occasion for him – and for that matter for others. He was to read a paper at a large and unprecedented international conference at the University, on some cures for speech defects. He wanted to spend his time until then restfully, composedly. There were one or two places in his paper where he could, he thought, make improvements. Nevertheless, this evening he had obeyed some nagging impulse, and an hour or so ago had set out from his hotel with the express purpose of picking somebody up.

. . . 'Why don't you sit down?' the young musician was saying to him in a changed, cheeky, alluring voice. 'It'd be a bloody sight more comfortable than hovering in front of me like someone looking at a caged bird at the zoo. I bet if I'd been the Spanish boy you first took me for, you'd have sat down beside me like a shot.'

Dan did as he had suggested, almost against his better judgement. Strange at this time of year to be able to sit outside at so late an hour: it was the latter half of November. No overcoat was necessary on this balmy evening. The tall plane-trees around them were touched only lightly by autumn, and Dan thought of their smaller London cousins, now naked and trembling in chilly wet winds. Above the white pseudo-Baroque towers and haughty rooftop statues of central Madrid the sky was like velvet.

'You really do play that harmonica of yours well,' he said, and once again in his mind there stood James, leaning against the wall of the back-garden of 'The Cedars', on the outskirts of Tanbury, a market-town in North Oxfordshire.

'That was your opening gambit,' said the young man. 'You surely can't have forgotten it already?'

'But it wasn't a gambit,' Dan protested, 'I meant what I said.' Perhaps I should tell him about James and about how the Bluegrass melody brought him back to me, he said to himself; perhaps I should tell him that in an hour's time it'll be James's birthday. But wouldn't that be manipulating pathos? 'You may think I'm kidding you,' he went on, 'but walking down the Paseo just now with all this going on,' and he gestured towards the noisy cars of the Franquistas, 'and then hearing your "Wildwood Flower" drifting down towards me . . . well, it moved me, I don't mind admitting it.'

A look first of surprise, then almost of gratitude came over the young man's face. 'So, you know the name of my tune?' he said, 'well, well, well! I'd never have expected it of you.' And he paused as if to give himself time to make sense of Dan's ability to recognise the melody. Then he said: 'No, I don't play badly, do I? But then, you see, I had a lot to do with someone who was a first-rate Bluegrass musician.'

Without Dan's having been aware he was doing so, he had moved up on the bench, with the result that his left thigh was now touching Dan's right. Dan did not withdraw; yesterday's air journey, today's tramp round a strange city had left him a little disorientated. Contact was therefore pleasing to him. In the lamplight the harmonica gleamed on its owner's lap like some luminous fish that he'd just caught. Dan could now make out one of the words engraved upon it: *Hohner*, the name of the make. James, he recalled, had always spoken highly of *Hohners*, though he couldn't quite remember why – something to do with their timbre. Underneath this, in matching germanic letters, but obviously more recently engraved, was another name – presumably the young man's – but this Dan could not read.

'What you're looking at,' said his bench-companion with a kind of throaty pride, 'this *Hohner*, is rather valuable, believe it or not. Made in . . . But you wouldn't be very interested in the details. They're meaningless except to other *aficionados*. But I will tell you something about this instrument, something that'll probably surprise you.' Once again he let the beams of his sloe-like eyes play upon Dan's face. 'It's my most prized possession. And I'll go nowhere without it. I love it for itself, and I love it for its personal associations. You see, it was a present from someone who means – no, *meant*, no means – such a lot to me.'

The fumblings in this last sentence made an appeal to the professional man in Dan. How often a patient began to trip over words, syllables, consonants when he was exposing an emotional nerve. 'Given to you?' he asked, 'By a lover of yours?'

'By a lover?' The astonishment in the young man's voice was obviously unfeigned. 'Me, the lover of . . .' But he could not, it would seem, bring himself to pronounce the all-important name. 'Oh, no, no, no, you've got things wrong there, my friend, very wrong.'

Dan now caught, from his new proximity to him, a whiff of his neighbour's breath. It smelt of whisky. Which made him think of poor old James once more.

'And I'll tell you something else,' the harmonica-player was continuing, 'for one minute I thought *you* were that someone who gave me the *Hohner*.'

'Me?'

'Yes, you. But don't worry – you don't really resemble or feature him much. You are dark, he's fair; you're a bit chunky in build, he's slender. But when you first appeared in front of me, there was just something about you, I can't say what, that reminded me. But I can't find it now. You've talked the resemblance away, I suppose.'

And across his gentle, sensual face, Dan saw pass swiftly a look of desolation. I know that look so well, he thought; how many times have I seen it on the faces of my patients at the clinic when dreaded memories suddenly surface.

'But this someone,' he said, 'even if he wasn't your lover – he was important to you, I take it?'

'Important? You can say that again,' the young man said with another bitter smile. 'Sometimes I can't remember my life before I knew him. But what interest can all this have for *you*? No more than the history of my harmonica. Because, don't let's kid ourselves,' and the truculent grin of earlier succeeded the tragical smile, 'you arrived in this little urban bower with one thing in your mind, didn't you? S.E.X., to put it crudely.'

It suddenly came to Dan that this particular young man, unlike some others, would be more wounded if he attempted to deny this statement than if he assented. 'Maybe, maybe,' he said, stifling a desire to say anything more committal, for really he did not know how he wanted to pass the night, and there was something disconcerting about his 'find'. Nevertheless – 'Don't you think we've been in this "urban bower" too long now?' he asked him. 'I can't say I care for our neighbours out in the roadway with all their commotion. I'd like to move on somewhere else. Wouldn't *you*?'

'To some gay club, you mean?' Yes, Dan *had* been right, the young man did seem reassured by his tacit acknowledgement of sexual interest. 'There are quite a number to choose from round here. You must already have sussed out how that labyrinth of old streets behind there,' and he pointed in front of him, away from the Paseo itself, 'contains one homosexual joint after another. For me it's great, just great, but you can't help wondering what Velázquez and Goya and all the other famous Spaniards of old would have made of it all, can you? But I expect many of them were saucy lads, and wouldn't have minded all that much.' He giggled – in a manner not wholly to Dan's taste. Indeed the whole naughty tone of these last remarks irked him somewhat. Made in Spanish, they might have been appealing, *gracioso*, but in his own tongue and accent . . . 'But perhaps you were inviting me back to your rooms?'

'I was thinking merely,' said Dan, 'of the two of us going across the road for a coffee in the *Gijón*.' He could see the lights of this most famous of Madrid cafés blazing appetisingly beyond the inner line of plane-trees. He had not yet visited it, and surely it would be a welcome contrast to the bellicose self-advertisements of the Franquistas on the road.

'To the *Gijón*, eh? To join all the artists chatting up the pretty-boys?'

'If that's what going there means.'

'I'll say it does. I don't know how many times I've hung round there to be stood coffees or drinks by interested parties. All *los intelectuales* of Madrid must have eyed me at one table or another. But don't get me wrong; I like the place, like it a lot.' He made no move to go, but smiled up at Dan somewhat disarmingly, almost innocently. And Dan was suddenly reminded of . . . of what, of whom? There had been, he thought, a photograph, back in Tanbury, one looked at affectionately by . . . But the association snapped. I am very tired after all, Dan thought, and my mind's probably playing me tricks.

Yet another volley of horn-signals broke out across the Paseo, and neither of the two acquaintances felt able to speak until it had ended. Then, still not budging from the bench, the younger said: 'I'm not quite the forced exile from our country that you're most likely thinking me, you know. I'm at home in this city; in fact you could say I'm practically a *Madrileño*.'

'You may be *at* home here, but *is* it your home?' asked Dan, visions of prosperous terraced houses in London coming, almost unbidden, into his mind.

'I don't believe in a home, my friend,' the young man was answering, 'I'd have thought *that* was clear about me. If it isn't, I don't know what else is, one thing excepted.'

Well, that makes two of us who don't believe in homes, Dan thought sadly, for it had not always been thus. There had been a time when he had not appreciated that the atmosphere of 'The Cedars' had denied him family life for ever.

'I was telling you,' the young man was going on, 'how often nowadays I can't remember life before I met the bloke who gave me the harmonica. Well, frequently I can't remember life before Madrid either. I love the place, and I don't just mean the sexual attractions of Chueca and this Paseo . . . There's the Metro, for example. You must already have seen all those dignified but cheerful students standing at the entrances to the underground stations selling off tickets they've bought in batches for the smallest of profits. I really take my hat off to them for their patience and for the way they stick together so loyally. And then the many people who all but live in the dirty marbled passageways leading to the platforms: legless musicians, bedraggled old women with begging daughters, hopeless-looking youths singing hopeful songs from Latin America to their guitars – every day I say to myself: You're all my cousins.'

He was, Dan noticed, pulling out of the right-hand pocket of his jeans – the bulge in which Dan had already felt against his leg – an old, black-leather box. In this he proceeded to lay, with the greatest tenderness, his *Hohner* harmonica. 'So,' he said, closing up the case with a little bang, 'maybe I ought to have answered you differently, and said that Madrid *is* a home for me, and I've no plans I know of for leaving it.'

And these ruthless rich young Franquistas, thought Dan, looking behind him at the Paseo, are *they* your cousins too?

'Come on,' he said, for he was a little bewildered by this sudden eulogy to the Spanish capital . . . 'Couldn't you do with some coffee yourself? After all your playing, and all your waiting?'

Their eyes met, and their doing so made Dan say: 'But before we go there, I *must* know your name. I can't spend the rest of the evening' (deliberately he did not say 'night') 'with someone completely identity-less.'

'Fair enough!' The musician smiled like the boy he must have surely been, charming, anxious to please . . . Yes, there *had* been a photograph somewhere. 'It's Kevin. But let's leave it at that, shall we, for now? I'd rather *not* give you my surname as well, it'd bring too many thoughts of England into my weary mind. And how about you? What's *your* name?'

'Dan.' This concealment of second names was maybe not such a bad idea, if an eccentric one.

'Pleased to meet you, Dan,' Kevin said, and he shook him by the hand with a surprising firmness.

The two of them got up from the bench and walked through the warm, clamorous, Spanish darkness to the Café *Gijón*.

2

An hour later Kevin was lying naked on top of the double bed in Dan's hotel-room, composing himself for the pleasurably charged moments before love-making began. Unswervingly he kept his eyes upon Dan who was still undressing, knowing, through experience, what the erotic impact of his intense, wondering expression would be. Concentration of regard also reduced awareness of the phoney luxury of the bedroom itself – walls covered in a furry-textured paper with a pseudo-Chinese pattern; an Anglepoise lamp resembling a frozen snake with a fierce bright head; an

overprominent fridge humming in remorseless announcement of
the hotel's ability to provide its guests with cosmopolitan liquor.
In how many different rooms had Kevin lain in just his present
attitude, and what a book he could write about them all – Gonzalo's scruffy one in an old street near Tirso de Molina, the walls
dingy and flaking, the dust in tangible chrysalises under the bed;
Fernando's book-lined one, where handsomely-bound editions of
Plato and other Greeks looked critically down from their shelves
at one's performance; the opulent room of Luis, his most persistent, his longest-standing admirer, who, after each night together,
would send Kevin a curiously formal but effusive thank-you letter:
'I know no other boy anywhere who can so beautifully satisfy me,'
etc. Oh, yes, with every person things were different, indeed every
time things were different. Each sexual experience had come to
seem to Kevin like sending a bucket for fresh water far down into
some deep well fed by secret and inexhaustible springs.

Second by second Dan was showing himself as even brawnier
than clothed he'd appeared to be; here and there he was perhaps a
little too fleshy for the most demanding standards, but on the whole
his body was vigorous-seeming, and youthful enough for Kevin
considerably to enjoy its uncovering. He was hairy too, particularly on the thighs. But there was something about his movements,
though suggestive of a certain physical competence – you could
imagine him playing a good game of squash – that indicated a lack
of *complete* self-confidence: this would surely show itself soon.
But, anyway, Kevin had already identified Dan's type over coffee
in the *Gijón*. In that crowded, square-shaped, panelled old café, lit
by globe-shaped bracketed lamps and curtained in deep maroon
velvet, conversation had not flowed at all well between them. Dan
had been a little disconcerted by the *Gijón's* more louche clientele,
and, too, by Kevin's obvious intimacy with it, his ability both to
talk and to gesture in its special, saucy, sexy language. Indeed it had
needed perseverance on Kevin's part for the half-hour in the café
not to end in a good-bye. But doubtful men often proved in the
end the most ardent lovers of them all.

Supine now on Dan's bed, Kevin amused himself by predicting
the course their love-making would follow. From the first Dan
would be tenderly attentive to Kevin's cock, but for some time

would be diffident of any reciprocal treatment; he would run eager, exploratory fingers down the crack in his arse for quite some minutes before venturing any penetration with tongue or member – and there would be points in the proceedings when the fervent, prolonged kiss would be more important for him than genital activity – though that too would have its own near-frenetic season. Then it would be that Kevin would hear profuse, impassioned compliments whispered into his ear – and questions too. Kevin had, from the time they met, *really* been attracted to him, hadn't he? He *was* enjoying himself now, wasn't he? He wasn't merely wanting to fill in an empty night, he wasn't wanting . . . Dan would not be able to bring himself to mention the word 'money', and Kevin himself deemed it best indeed not to raise that delicate matter until latish the next morning.

Tony and Rob; Chris, Ian and Peter; that interesting nameless man in Marseilles; Julio and Gonzalo and Fernando and Luis – unalike in character, background, lifestyle, had all been almost comically alike in their compliments to Kevin. 'Mysterious', 'fascinating', beautiful', even 'good, and I *mean* good!' And doubtless Dan would pay him some, if not all, of these tonight. Of course they were deserved; the man was lucky who got Kevin. Before they went to sleep, Dan would say to him: 'I can't believe my luck in coming across *you* – by *chance!* – in the Paseo. It almost makes me believe in Destiny.' As if he hadn't been on the look-out for a youth, and Kevin hadn't been loitering on a bench there waiting for a man.

Sometimes, when slipping into sleep, Kevin would feel deliciously cocooned by satisfaction, always endorsed by the grateful caresses of his partners. And in such a cocoon he would, on happy occasions, dream of the one person who *had* deeply delighted him, though they had never made love, would dream of that person as he'd been before his tragedy. Golden-haired, with eyes of cornflower-blue, he stood in a September garden and played the harmonica, all the reddening trees and imminently departing birds responding, it had appeared, to the beauty of his tunes. And later this friend would be taking him once again to Tanbury Fair, with its great Ferris wheel brilliant above the houses of the market square, or into Foxton woods – the two of them making a way through willowherb and ferns to a spot by a moss-banked stream where they might – if they were very fortunate – catch a glimpse of badgers.

Never at such times did Kevin dream about his own part in that dear friend's downfall, nor about how he had looked when he'd seen him last, staring terribly into Nothing. But on waking, alas, he would remember these, and then everything, even the renewed embraces of his bed-companion, would seem foreign and cold.

When Dan, after turning off the bedroom light, came to him, he was very good to touch and smell. Still composed, but with desire pushing its strong current to his loins, Kevin put hands upon matted chest, stiff cock, tight scrotum, hirsute thighs, and sensed, behind them all, need, uncertainty, kindness of intent, a tense appreciation of himself. And who's better than me at giving ease, said Kevin to himself. Now Dan's mouth was upon his own, discandying upon his tongue delight and – yes, affectionate respect. Respect? That was a response he *was* in need of; his compulsively promiscuous life didn't solicit it often. In gratitude, Kevin worked his much-practised tongue against Dan's with a gentle energy.

Things proceeded between them more or less as Kevin had inwardly forecast. Dan resembled Tony and that man in Marseilles. He made love enthusiastically, and all the time you were aware of a strength in both his body and his spirit – also of a certain unappeased hunger. He lived alone, Kevin could tell; nor did he have sex with someone every night or even every other night! Behind his postures and actions there was an emotional loneliness to be felt. His 'form' was not very sophisticated; indeed it was somewhat disappointing in its lack of that inventiveness Kevin had become accustomed to in his partners. He needed guiding into the most physically exciting positions, ones that seemed never to have occurred to him. But, provided he was encouraged with hotly whispered remarks about how *simpático* he was, he seemed very pleased to be guided.

It was well past two o'clock – and Kevin, for his part, could have gone on for some while longer – when they stopped making love. The room was then all at once restored to its bleak, pretentious self; dark though it was, the forms of intertwined dragons showed unpleasantly again on the furry walls, and the humming of the fridge, obliterated by sexual activity, became all-too-audible once more: 'You're back in the world of things, of things, of *things!*' it seemed to be saying. Kevin turned over on to his left side; he had known warmer self-generated cocoons because he'd known more adventurous lovers. On the other hand – and Dan's arms were round him now, his head gentle and reposeful upon his back – he had known few as nice. *Few?* . . . *None* as nice, it suddenly seemed. It was Sunday now; on Monday Dan would read his paper on speech defects at the *Universidad Complutense*, and then, late that afternoon, he'd fly back to England, that country Kevin had forsworn for ever. Of course Kevin didn't look for permanence, even for longevity, in his relationships; he wasn't some romantic-minded innocent! All the same it was a pity this one had to be quite so short-lived.

Dan's lips were giving his back a gentle, good-night kiss.

'You liked me?' Kevin whispered. He always wanted to hear praise of himself. When he was low, he'd repeat to himself tributes he'd received.

'Haven't I made that clear? And you me?'

'Of course!' Kevin moved his body so that, still lying in an embrace, their heads were now cheek to cheek upon the bank of pillows. This bed was a great deal more comfortable than his own in his squalid little room in the Calle de San Marcos. It was adequate compensation for the wallpaper and the fridge. Suddenly a wave of curiosity about this man beside him broke over him. What questions he had asked Dan back in the *Gijón* had been more a means of making him feel wanted, of flattering him into going ahead with an invitation for the night, than of gratifying interest on his own part. But now he wanted Dan's niceness to be in some way accounted for. What had he been like when younger? What had produced this sympathetic blend of concern and independence from conventionality?

'Tell me more about yourself, Dan,' he said, stressing the Christian name and caressing the folds of skin on the back of his neck.

'But what sort of things would you want to know? Anyway I'd rather learn about you than talk about myself.'

'Oh, I'm not worth expending much curiosity on,' Kevin said hastily. 'I've got a foolish nature and a butterfly mind – as many a person has told me. And where I've sprung from couldn't be less interesting; anyway, as I've already told you, I've left it behind.' But was anywhere completely without interest? he asked himself. And the terraced house in Lewisham arose before him. Gerald, his father, was late home – taking a woman other than Kevin's mother out to dinner again? Or maybe Dad *was* at home, in his study, pursuing the one serious interest his position as head of a large advertising agency hadn't been able to suppress: Spanish history. Volumes on *Los Reyes Católicos* or the exploits of the Extremaduran *Conquistadores* lay open on the desk before him. And here was Christina, Kevin's mother, trailing through rooms in her kimono-like housegown, all but wringing her hands and saying: 'Heaven knows I have tried to be a good wife to your father, Kevin. Why, I've even read books on how to be a successful hostess! For *his* sake, of course!' Then another house became almost as distinct – St. Jude's Vicarage in Tanbury, Oxfordshire, where lived his father's brother and sister; Father Edward Lalland, former member of the Community of the Resurrection at Mirfield, Anglo-Catholic, animal-lover; and the gentle, grave Frances Lalland, authoress of two books on needlecraft: *Embroidery Ellen* and *Patchwork Polly*. What a far cry from cruisers and traders in Chueca, Madrid!

Kevin forced himself away from his quick succession of mental pictures, and said: 'What I'd like to hear about, Dan, is your early days – before you were my age even, all those centuries ago.' And to know why you're gay, he nearly added, and then thought better of it. He tickled Dan's neck, and as he spoke those last teasing words, he made, even in the darkness, a pretty little moue such as had always antagonised his father.

As he'd expected, Dan was not really very unwilling to supply information about himself.

'I don't suppose I was quite what you imagine me now,' he said, 'what I think of as my real self took some time in becoming dominant. It was a very difficult business coming to terms with my home. Well,' and he gave rather a mirthless laugh, 'I wonder if my brother and I have *ever* come truly to terms with it, or if we will ever do so. Just when we think we've put it behind us, it asserts itself again.'

I don't think that's at all true about me, Kevin said to himself;

I've been able to forget home pretty easily all things considered. What would be stranger than to see my mother walking through the streets of Chueca? Except to see my father propping up one of its gay bars. 'Where *was* this home?' he asked.

'On the outskirts of a country town in the Midlands.'

Kevin murmured knowingly; of course he was seeing, in his mind's eye, Tanbury. For all its 'olde-worlde' charm – the market-place, the parish church, the chestnut-lined Horse Fair – it would be a dull place to grow up in.

'It was the home itself, however, not its situation that was the trouble. Though if it had been situated in London rather than in the rural Midlands, it perhaps would have been a little less claustrophobic.

'I had one great companion, though – my brother. He and I did everything together. I don't think either of us would have imagined that our ways would diverge one day quite radically . . .'

'But they did?'

'Oh, yes, they did all right!' Kevin heard a distinct sadness in Dan's voice. 'Though both of us obviously still remember all we shared.'

'What sort of things?' Being an only child Kevin had many times felt that his life would have run a very different course had he had a companion close to him in spirit and years within the house. Someone with whom he could forget Daddy's adulteries and ennui, Mummy's melancholia and self-pity.

'Walking, roaming round the countryside. Observing birds and animals.'

And things would have been different too, thought Kevin, if he had been able to enjoy the countryside when adolescent. London had been too full too early of pairs of older eyes shining with desire.

'I suppose the most remarkable activity my brother and I under-took together was badger-watching. I doubt if you've ever done it, or know even how one goes about it. Somehow I imagine you a real townee.'

What was it he was hearing? *Badger-watching!* Had he ever done it, indeed? Did he know how you went about it? And even as he framed a reply to Dan's unjust remarks, a terrible possibility – no, maybe more, a likelihood – came into Kevin's head. Cold hands of fear clutched him.

'Not that I didn't have friends other than my brother in my town,' Dan was saying. 'I did have. Two great friends, in fact. First Richard – he still is a very good friend to me, and he will, as it happens, be in Madrid tomorrow evening. And then there was Jason – though he and I, to all intents and purposes, broke with one another after . . .' He left the sentence unfinished.

So now we have Jason, Kevin said to himself. An uncommon name in Dan's generation! No doubt of it. He was about to be plunged into that goldfish bowl of which he'd spoken so bitterly back on the Recoletos. A bowl the waters of which were poisoned, making the fish come to the surface eager for gulps of air, but dying nonetheless.

'But my brother meant more to me than anyone,' Dan was continuing.

'Tell me,' said Kevin, his voice sounding, he thought, surprisingly normal and free from anxiety in the circumstances, 'tell me about the house you lived in when you were young.'

Dan gave vent to something that was part sigh, part laugh. 'The house I lived in when I was young,' he said, 'you couldn't predict it in a month of Sundays, Kevin. Outwardly it wasn't so very extraordinary – a Victorian villa at the edge of the town; it was built of red brick, dulled with the weather, and had mock-ecclesiastical windows. It usually looked rather shabby, though after my mother's death, my brother did his best to keep it orderly, and to make improvements in it. He was/is very practical.'

The cocoon had well and truly slipped from Kevin now.

'But inside was another story. I'll open the front door and you can judge for yourself. Ahead of you on the far wall of the hall you would have seen two really enormous gilt-framed oil paintings: they made a pair. The landscape was the same in each – rocky mountains, olive trees, bits of classical temples. The left-hand picture showed a band of tall, proud, flaxen-haired youths setting off on a Marathon across the country; the right-hand picture depicted the crowning of the victor of this race by some toga-clad general. The painter's name – you won't have heard of it – was Friedrich Mayerhofer. Those pictures could have told you a lot about our household, but I don't know how many people learned from them. Except of course Jason. And he . . .' Once again Dan did not finish his sentence; it would, Kevin thought, have been odd if he had.

Tranquil Tranquil Kevin advised himself. In his darkest recent imaginings he had never anticipated *this!*

Then he felt Dan squeeze his arm, and say in a sad, imploring voice: 'Kevin, I can't go on with this account of the past, I really can't. Don't ask me why; I have good reasons.'

I've no need to ask you why, my friend, Kevin said wryly to himself. Though of course what *you* know and what *I* know about the whole terrible affair may be very different. Why, he wondered, had he not tumbled earlier to Dan's identity? Out in that bower in the Paseo, he had surely been given all the clues: that fleeting resemblance he himself had noticed, Dan's recognition of 'Wildwood Flower'.

Dan, of course, was misinterpreting Kevin's silence. 'I'm sorry,' he said, 'I shouldn't have embarked on a description of my background only to say that I couldn't continue. You'll think I don't trust you with details about my life, and that isn't the case at all.' He spoke nervously, like a much younger man.

'Oh, I understand about it better than you think,' said Kevin truthfully, 'look, don't let's discuss it any more. We *both* must be exhausted now; neither of us has exactly been inactive. Let's get some sleep.' Some chance, he added to himself.

With slow deliberation Kevin turned away from Dan, upon his left side. Their love-making seemed all at once as firm in an unrepeatable past as those events in Tanbury last year.

It was not very long, however, before he felt Dan's lips pressing upon his back.

'You like me?'

'Of course.'

'Could you . . . *love* me?'

'Perhaps,' said Kevin, exhaustedly, warily, 'and now let me go to sleep, please, Dan!'

3

Of the two old friends of his that Dan had mentioned to Kevin, Richard Cardew was, as he'd implied, also in Spain, staying the night with a professor at Salamanca University and his family. From the windows of their long, whitewashed farmhouse the city itself could be seen, mounted on the bluffs of its river, soaring yet solid, as if composed of giant golden stalactites. The Olmedo family ate late – the Professor himself had prepared the *paella valenciana*, its rice a brilliant saffron yellow in which shellfish and prawns hid as they might on some beach. And as they ate the professor told his English friend and associate a story of his own boyhood.

He had been living then in a town in Murcia which fell, not from its own sympathies but from its geographical inadequacies, to Franco and his Moorish troops. Walking in the main street a few days after the surrender, Antonio had encountered two members of these last – tall, grinning men who had proceeded, with simulated friendliness, to waylay him. What, they had asked, did he think of the new arrivals? – better than the rabble-like Republican lot, eh? They could provide great times for the youth of the district. Why didn't Antonio accompany them now to the house where they were quartered? This had been really more a command than an invitation, and Antonio had realised he had no alternative but to do what they said.

The house had been itself ordinary enough – indeed it had been requisitioned from a man Antonio knew, a communist schoolmaster who was now God-only-knew-where – probably dead! What they wanted to show him, the taller, the more constantly grinning of the two men had said, was situated on the top storey: Antonio must follow them. When they'd climbed up all the stairs, the same man had told him: 'Look at the view, won't you? You'll like it.' And, before Antonio could appreciate what was happening to him, the two soldiers had seized hold of him and dragged him roughly, jeeringly over to the window. They'd then gripped his ankles with powerful hands and dangled him from it, knocking his head many times against the house walls.

'So for twenty minutes of my life the world was upside down for me, and I think that with one eye, in all the subsequent years, I always saw it so. That is perhaps why I turned to Language, to the brain's attempt to impose order on the world. That is why of all Spanish poets I have admired Pedro Salinas the most, because of his metaphysical explorations of grammar.'

Richard thought of his own quiet growing-up in Tanbury, Oxfordshire, and shuddered. But even there the world could be turned upside down. As in the Varney household.

That evening Jason Fletcher, who was Literary and Arts Editor of the magazine *Project*, had deputised for its theatre critic and attended the first night of a foolish play about the French Revolution. He arrived home at his flat behind Notting Hill Gate in a bad mood; intellectual dishonesty and artistic stupidity always enraged him, had indeed obsessively done so since his precocious youth. Sorrel, his wife, was sitting at her work-table, engrossed in the illustrations she had undertaken for a children's book. Patiently, under the light of a white-shaded lamp, she was making 'roughs' for a drawing of two mice quarrelling over a lump of cheese. How calm she looked, how prettily her long, loose, chestnut-coloured hair glinted in the lamplight. Nevertheless Jason broke into her calm:

'Well, darling, I've had a wonderful time! I only wish you could have been there to share the mental exhilaration, the emotional stimulus with me. Well – Julian Beckett obviously doesn't know what he's perpetrated, but he will – he will.'

'Julian Beckett?' said Sorrel, her pencil playing with the mountainous morsel of cheese.

'The author of the great play.'

'Oh, Jason,' said Sorrel, smiling winningly up at him, 'you aren't going to be in one of your hostile, I'll-get-them moods, are you?'

'I shall in my article make play with his name,' Jason said, ignoring this, taking off his smart, fur-collared coat and throwing it on to the sofa, 'I shall compare him with his namesake Samuel Beckett. I shall write – in Swiftian style – about tonight's wretched, romantically royalist piece of boulevard nonsense as if I were discussing *End Game* or *Krapp's Last Tape*. That should show him, that should teach him never to put pen to paper again!'

And then he remembered a certain article of his, equally unsparing, which had appeared in *The Observer* a year ago tomorrow, and what pain it had brought, and wondered if he should not let his wrath be confined to rhetorical outbursts to Sorrel. He went up to her, tenderly kissed the top of her head, and then looked over her hair at her sketches on the table-top.

'They're *very* good, sweetheart,' he said warmly, 'though I think the mice look a *little* bit too much like you and me!'

'They don't, do they?' said Sorrel anxiously, 'they weren't meant to!'

'Well, so I should hope. But I've entered the depths of your creative being, you see, and I know there'll be no cure for you. A mouse, a walrus, a pterodactyl, they'll all have your husband's face. As for the cheese, it looks like a furniture removal van, a pantechnicon.'

'You're apprehensive about Monday's move, aren't you?'

'Probably,' said Jason.

'Shall I make us some cocoa? You seem to need soothing.'

'That'd be very welcome.'

'By the way,' Sorrel said, 'there's a letter for you. The postman delivered it to the flat downstairs by mistake, and Mr Evans brought it up earlier this evening.'

The Kenilworth postmark at first perplexed Jason. Then he realised whom it could be from, and a trepidation seized him. He was to be proved right in his deduction.

'*Dear Jason,*' he read, and the pulse beat painfully behind each eye,

'*Eleven months later might seem a weird time to thank someone for a Christmas card. But then I've been officially designated a weirdo, haven't I? – not least, thanks to you. The fact is I was tidying out my desk-drawer before leaving this snug little place in which I've been incarcerated for so long. And I came across your kind seasonal greeting. Why hadn't I chucked it into the waste-paper basket the moment I got it? I asked myself. Or better, torn it up and thrown the pieces down the bog? I certainly didn't feel like replying to the card. But now I do. What made you want to communicate with me, Jason? Your usual inability to leave things alone? Or maybe – one can always hope – guilt?*

'*I'd like to make you realise what I think about you. For me things are now no different from what they were on Dan's seventeenth birthday. I know you won't have forgotten that fight we had that day in the cricket-pavilion after you'd insulted Pappa. I'd like to fight you again, to bring my fist hard against your face. You were meant to come round for a birthday supper that night. For obvious reasons you didn't. When the rather melancholy meal was over, Dan and I went up to Foxton Woods and sat there by the badgers' sett, and Dan told me about badgers being given ritual burial by their own kind, with rabbits as gravediggers. I've always remembered that piece of information; somehow it's been a comfort to me.*

'*One hour in Foxton Woods is worth several life-times in your company.*

'*With no good wishes,*

'*James Varney.*'

'Was that letter anything important, pet?' called out Sorrel from the kitchen.

'No,' replied Jason after a brief pause, 'nothing important at all.' In one sense, he'd spoken the truth – disturbing, yes, but how could it, in any way, be 'important'? *Now!*

'Pappa', Hampton Varney, with his leonine white-haired head, Hampton Varney dead through a heart attack six months ago, suddenly stood before Jason as he'd never done in real life. Behind him, in the oppressive drawing-room of 'The Cedars', with its heroic pictures and knobbly old furniture, was the glass-fronted book-case with the shelf containing what he liked to call 'The Mighty Handful', the man's entire published *oeuvre*. The shelf began with the privately printed *Oxfordshire Sap – a Rhapsody on Rural Themes* (actually he had been *J*. Hampton Varney then) and proceeded through the novels – *The Sacrament of Grass*; *The Nettle Safety, the Rose Danger*; *I Hear a Hero Calling* – to various ephemera, quasi-political pamphlets like *Shaking Germany by the Hand* and *Recovering the Slumbering Will*. And now to this row could be added last year's glossy paperback edition of *The Sacrament of Grass* (a *Proxima Centauri Press* publication) about which Jason had written so many stinging words. And what about the work he had left behind him: *Prospero; a Shakespearean Romance*, which had been entrusted – an odd choice – not to his sons, but to Father Edward Lalland, his literary executor?

Jason wondered what Hampton Varney would say, could he know his and Sorrel's destination on Monday morning.

'Jason, darling, shall we have some nice ginger biscuits with our cocoa?' Sorrel was asking him.

Dan couldn't but remember that he'd asked many boys in bed these last years: 'Could you . . . *love* me?' Quite often they'd said: 'Yes!', and even when their replies had been rather more non-committal they'd hinted at futures to be in some way shared with him. But the sad fact remained that none of his affairs had ever developed into the desired, committed partnership. Oh, yes, out of these consummated, romantic nights friendships had come, and ones he valued. But that was something quite different.

What reason had he now to think that he had met the one young man who could command both his heart and his body, and who would bestow upon him his own? What qualities had emanated from Kevin's embraces and kisses, or from his eyes as they had shone searchingly upon him in the darkness of the room, to make him think: my agreeing to speak at this conference in Madrid may well turn out to be the happiest decision of my life? Perhaps it was destructive to try so much as to name these qualities – 'we murder to dissect', after all. Of one thing, however, Dan was certain: the love-making would have gone quite differently, indeed the whole encounter would have been altogether otherwise, if he had not beforehand heard Kevin play the harmonica. If he had not been moved to track down the boy who was rendering 'Wildwood Flower' as lyrically, as ardently as James himself.

And now, of course, it was inevitable that his mind travelled back to James again. Tomorrow – no, *today* (for it was two and a half hours past midnight) – his brother would be thirty-six years old. 'Don't, for Christ's sake, come bothering me about my birthday, will you?' James had said to him at their last meeting (one proposed and then insisted upon by Dan). 'You're not fool enough to imagine I'll be celebrating it, are you?'

Dan was still joyously aware of Kevin's fragrant, erotic proximity, apart though they now had drawn. His right foot rested upon Dan's left . . . James's birthday! Dan tried to think of a pleasant predecessor for this one, but the only birthday clear in his memory was his own seventeenth, a day, he knew, James himself would not have forgotten.

The weather that day had been of the kind celebrated by the medieval carollers of May: the hawthorn blossom had been profuse on bushes and hedgerows like some fall of scented snow, the leaves on the trees a delicate, fresh green. But in fact terrible things had happened during its course: the fight between James and Jason in the cricket pavilion after the afternoon match; his own learning from the lips of Father Lalland the truth behind life at 'The Cedars'. And the celebrations planned had, on account of these, not taken place.

But the sun had not gone down on unrelieved misery. For James and himself it had descended behind the Cotswolds as seen from Foxton Woods, while they were waiting for the badgers to lumber streamwards. Recalling that night, Dan could smell again the wild garlic and sorrel, feel the briars brushing and scraping against him, and hear all those multitudinous sounds of a wood at night; the chimes of the rivulets and the stream, the scamperings and rustlings underfoot, the hootings and shrillings overhead.

They had been sitting together in silence for some time, before James had said: 'Look, Dan, I brought this with me!' And he'd pulled out of his jeans pocket the harmonica he'd bought a few months back at one of the stalls in Tanbury market. 'I'd like to compete with the birds for a few minutes. I've been learning a really great American tune. From the mountains in the Land of the Free – over there!' (He'd pointed to the now black outlines of the Cotswolds with the sun sinking behind them.) 'It's called "Wildwood Flower" – rather suitable don't you think?' He'd placed his instrument to his lips. As he'd done so, a shaft of new moonlight had caught it, making it glint so that to Dan the sweetly billowing melody issuing from it had been made up of light as well as of sound. And it had seemed to him also that all the secret lives of the wood – the owls, the ferns, the weasels, the briar-roses, the rushes down by the stream, the invisible, elusive badgers, and Dan himself – had quivered at James's musical consummations.

And only a few hours ago, in so very unlikely a place, Dan had heard 'Wildwood Flower' – and played in a similar fashion – again.

Kevin was asleep now. The face that, only a short while back, had been alight with mischievous sexy merriment, resembled now some prelapsarian animal's. It was not Dan but innocence itself that was caressing it, that was indeed cradling his whole body. Dan longed to kiss him again; but it would, of course, be selfish of him to do so.

To avoid further temptation, Dan moved himself some inches apart from him. Firmly he shut his eyes. Recently he had found sleep hard. He tried to enter it now by means of pleasing thoughts. Tomorrow morning he would wake up to find an interesting, beautiful young man beside him. They would make love again – if not full consummation, then a lying tight in one another's arms that was, in its own way, as delectable. Then *together* they would get up, and *together* they would have breakfast. Easy with one another, they would talk – discover tastes, prejudices, hopes, conclusions about life and human nature in common. The past need not be mentioned.

But now down the corridors upon which his closed eyes had opened the Franquistas of the Paseo were making their way. Once more they were brandishing flags with wanton enthusiasm from speedy, predatory cars. 'What does it feel like to *be* them?' Kevin had wondered, as well he might. For how *did* they view themselves, and how did they name, let alone explain the lusts so transparently possessing them?

When Dan fell asleep, it was upon his back, a bad position. It was not surprising, perhaps, that among his dreams there was one which took him to Foxton Woods.

Once again he trod through them towards the stream, only there was no James at his side now. He was alone, and over the woodland, and indeed over the country beyond it, a heavy silence prevailed. And when he reached the stream, he realised that it too was making no sound as it flowed clear over pebbles and over larger, moss-covered stones. Dan stood by its banks for a moment, wondering at the absence of noise, the absence of any signs of life. And then he saw, floating upon the stream like a rotten log, a human form.

The current swirled this into the line of fuller vision, revealing it to be the body of Pappa – dressed, as he so often had been, in shapeless corduroys and shaggy fisherman's sweater, and dead – with cold, unseeing eyes turned skywards. I shouldn't let him float on, should I? Dan thought; the least I can do for him is to pull him on to the bank and then give him a proper burial.

He searched for a long stick and found, a few inches from his feet, a fallen branch. This he proceeded to cast into the stream like a fisherman his rod. As he caught hold of the body, it, to his irritation, keeled over upon the crystalline surface of the water. And instead of seeing the back of his father, Dan saw to his amazement and horror the front of his brother – wearing blue jeans and a red-and-black checked shirt. He – once again the eyes told you so – was ineluctably dead too! 'James!' he shouted, *'James!'*

He must have cried his brother's name out loud. He woke up, with his throat sore, as if after screaming. He was in Foxton Woods no longer, had, of course, seen neither his father nor James, was instead gazing up at a dark, alien ceiling. Why, of course, he realised sadly, I'm in a Spanish hotel, the Hotel San Bernardo, and James – though presumably at this very moment asleep – is still in his Hades-like land of shadows. But there *was* something else, something to be pleased about. He remembered Kevin.

Surreptitiously he extended a hand towards his bed-companion who, while he'd been having his dream, had rolled yet further away from him. But the hand did not encounter the boy. He must have gone to the bathroom, Dan thought; perhaps it was his getting out of bed, in fact, which had woken him up. He leaned over and switched on the bedside lamp. 'Kevin?' he called. But he was nowhere to be seen – empty bed, empty room, and the bathroom door was open, showing that *that* part of the suite was empty also.

Something very like fear seized Dan. He got out of bed and, pointlessly, examined every corner of the rooms as if Kevin had been a kitten who could conceal himself in strange places. He even opened the door into the passage, and peered down it. Had the youth been a figment of his imagination? Had he made love with him only in his mind? Then he noticed that on top of the gleaming, humming fridge was an object not put there by himself. There could be no mistaking it! It was the black case which contained

Kevin's *Hohner* harmonica. Which proved surely that Dan had *not* invented the visitor to these rooms?

But why had Kevin gone? And why had he left behind what he'd already described, in that lamplit bower in the Recoletos, as his 'most prized possession'?

Dan picked up the case – almost as if it were some religious relic, as perhaps in a sense it was – and opened it. The silver fish shone at him. And then he saw the personal name engraved upon its back, in Gothic lettering to match the trademark. It was the name of his own only brother, James Varney.

4

Up and up and up they went, the steep stone stairs of the old building in the Calle de San Marcos where Kevin lived. His land-lord, a fat, morose man from a former Spanish Saharan colony, had made out of the attic storey no fewer than sixteen bed-sitting-rooms, little, cheap, wretched affairs which would have been called cell-like had it not been for the extraordinary panoramas their windows commanded – of a rooftop universe of tiles, guttering, pigeons, T.V. aerials, chimneys like segments of Cubist paintings, and, pressing down upon everything, the sky.

Kevin's room contained a bed, a cupboard for his clothes, a small table with a crudely bright formica top, a couple of chairs, a diminutive electric stove, an equally diminutive fridge, and a washbasin. (Bath and lavatory, both invariably squalid, he shared with other occupants of the top storey.) He had, of course, tried to make the room reflect his personality – just a little. For example, in front of the window he had placed pots of yellow, pink and blue primulas, and had hung a cage in which a very red canary hopped about, like an extracted heart that could sing. On the walls were posters of art exhibitions in the galleries of the Calles Claudio Coello and Velázquez, and also brightly toned ones of pop heroes: so that all the time he was in his flat there stared down at him – Ry Cooder; Bob Dylan (at various stages of his life); Miguel Bosé, so incredibly desirable, with that scarlet bullfighter's scarf of his gracing his forehead; and of course, who else but David Bowie,

'King of Gay Power'? He'd also put up some sketches of Marilyn
Monroe done by himself from photographs. There were paperbacks – books on folk music, gay sex and animals, some detective
stories and some secondhand volumes of Spanish poetry: Lorca,
Jiménez etc., of which, truth to tell, he'd managed to read only a
few pages. And there were photographs – ten or twelve showing
himself in various different appealing attitudes; in some pictures
he was alone, in others he stood beside an English admirer – Theo,
Lewis, Vincent, Michael. And there were two of James, of James
Varney. How fine he looked, with his blue eyes shining out from
his bony strong face into the camera that Kevin was holding, and
defying anyone to guess how grimly clouded they would become.
(There was no photograph of Jason Fletcher.)

'It's me talking to you once again, James,' Kevin said aloud
to him, 'you more than anyone would know what it feels like to
have to live in a place like this. Didn't you tell me about dumps
you'd lived in yourself? And you, more than anyone also, must
know what it feels like to dread the prospect of the day ahead.
Not to mention the week or the month! I often gabble on to you
like this, don't I? Imagining you as you were when I took those
snaps, forgetting that you must look very different now, and that
you never answered that letter I wrote you! Anyway, today I've got
news for you: James, I've just made love with your brother – yes,
he's a gay like me! And I've left him as a souvenir the harmonica,
the precious harmonica you gave me that terrible day. But having
parted with it is like having parted from *you* a *second* time. Oh,
James, you were the sun in my life and now it seems as if you've
finally gone out.'

On arriving at his flat – at five o'clock in the morning – Kevin
had straightaway undressed and gone to bed. Now five hours later
he didn't feel like getting up. Because what was there to get up *for*?
Kevin turned over in bed, as he might have done to please a lover,
as he had indeed done for Daniel Varney last night, and like a child
(though in point of fact not like the child he himself had been; he
had been cheerful, high-spirited) he sobbed and sobbed into his
pillow.

And the tears became an element through which a compulsively
resurrected James now moved, in happy attitudes, ones which

had once filled Kevin, the onlooker, with the sheerest delight but which, this morning, could only exacerbate his distress. In the shimmering, salty world between eyeballs and closed, sore lids James stood once more on the porch of 'The Cedars', the music of his harmonica making the rambling roses that covered the porch roof shake; once more the two of them were picking apples, plums, nuts, pears; once more James was saying to him: 'Kiddo, I think you've got what it takes to be a really ace Bluegrass musician. If you'll let me teach you, you'll soon be playing "Johnny's Down the River" and "Down Yonder" and "Raggerty Annie" with the best of them!' The very names of the tunes had seemed then to Kevin like passports to a world of enchantment.

And, in so far as he'd glimpsed such a world this fraught last year, it surely *had* been through playing such melodies, and in the way James had shown him. How on earth had James survived without his beloved instrument? 'Harmonica's Bridegroom' – that had been, Kevin had learned, a local's name for him. Should he, he'd often wondered, have allowed himself to receive the gift of his friend's bride?

Outside the windows of Kevin's room white pigeons strutted on red tiles against an unadulteratedly blue sky, issuing, as they did so, curious croupy chortles. Perhaps they were envious of the safety of the cagebird they could see within. For its part Kevin's canary delivered itself, on seeing the outsiders, of a few plaintive notes – *it* was envious of *them*. So there it is, Kevin told himself, no one's in the right place. James hadn't been and wasn't. He himself hadn't been and wasn't. Lewisham, the offices of the magazine *Project*, Tanbury, they had all become at some point intolerable to him, caging him in frustration and guilt. Which indeed could and did still plague him in far-away Madrid!

Jason Fletcher; *he* was the one to blame, wasn't he? For so much of the time now Kevin hated him, hated, too, the relationship he had had with him.

Yet he had not always done so! On the contrary, there had been a time when he'd thought association with Jason Fletcher the greatest fortune that had ever come his way. He would even bring Jason presents – a bottle of wine, a box of candied fruits, a pomegranate, some persimmons – as an expression of this feeling.

In Madrid there hadn't been real rain ever since he'd come here. Kevin wished it *would* rain, not just because it would so relieve the worried Madrileños – though that, he hastily said to himself, must be his principal reason for wanting it – but because it would complement certain feelings of his as smiling sun in unclouded sky could not. Nevertheless he felt the rebuke of that sun now. He must not go on lying in bed alone. He must force himself outwards and forwards – to places which now seemed permanent parts of both his geographical and his emotional landscapes.

First he would take himself to that new but already infamous sauna where one day, a week or so ago, he'd spent five hours receiving the attention of a succession of men! Then he'd meet some of his mates for a beer and a snack; most of these friends lived as he did, and with them he enjoyed a *camaraderie* he'd never known before. For the young *maricones* of Chueca were lightly solicitous of each other in a way Kevin found both touching and reassuring. And as for the evening – well, to a club, of course. To the *Viznaga*, perhaps, with its pounding music and flashing lights and dancing youths watching both themselves and the effect they made on others in the large ceiling-to-floor mirrors! Or to the snootier *Phalo* with its erotic drawings on the wall and hirsute barmen wearing minimal clothing like captive cavemen.

Anyway, Kevin said to himself, I'll have to go to one of these places because once more I'm low on cash. For he had not – for obvious reasons – asked Dan Varney for money.

5

'It seems like it's the end of the world, doesn't it?' said the girl, sitting opposite him. She had a freckled face and long brown hair, and she was speaking about the driving rain on the other side of the train window obscuring the countryside beyond. 'They always say it'll rain for weeks before the end comes, you know.'

Do they? Who? James Varney wondered. Presumably she was referring to something like the Book of Revelation, though in her thick, oatmeal jersey and light-blue, tight-fitting jeans she didn't look at all a religious type.

'Oh, I shouldn't worry; I expect the world'll go on turning for quite some time yet,' James answered in a hearty tone. The girl couldn't possibly know what a nerve she'd touched with her remark. One of the most persistent images that had come to him when he was 'very bad', as he now called it, had been of the world as an orange, as in some primary-school teacher's geography lesson, of an orange shrivelling before his horrified eyes until it fell, miserable, stinking bit of rubbish, into the shapeless black cave of Space. But no more thoughts of *ends* of worlds, he rebuked himself; today must be looked at as the beginning of one. No sooner had he said this to himself, than, glancing out through the grubby, rain-scoured pane at the forlorn Midlands landscape – that more familiar to him than any other, but today very nearly unrecognisable – he felt the old terror rising up within him.

'So where are you off to this fine Sunday morning?' the girl was asking him with a cheery smile. She pulled over to her lap a large plastic bag out of which she took a small orange unpleasantly similar to that in James's fantasy.

'Tanbury.'

'Tanbury; well, what a coincidence; that's where *I'm* going too!'

It wasn't a coincidence at all, of course. The likelihood of their both having Tanbury as their destination on this particular train, and at this particular stage in its journey, was surely very high indeed. The girl was really quite pretty, James thought, in an ingenuous, composed way. He liked her budlike mouth and her small nose and her long brown lashes, and the air of good health that even in this damp, dirty carriage hung about her. She certainly was a contrast to the girls with dérangé eyes and bodies either upsettingly skeletonic or else sluggish with too much pill-taking, sleep, and nervous eating, with whom he'd been perforce associating for so long.

'Tanbury's such an important place these days, isn't it?' the girl was saying.

James could scarcely believe his ears. *Important? Tanbury?* There had been many times in his life when he had wondered whether there could be anywhere duller. His parents in 'The Cedars', he'd sometimes imagined, had taken hold of Time and administered chloroform to him, so that they could go on with their eventless, measureless way of life – Pappa taking himself to his study every morning and out across the fields every afternoon, to write and to ponder on his 'masterpiece', *Prospero*, a romance about Shakespeare and the writing of *The Tempest*. While Mamma cooked nuts and nettles and nasturtium roots in the damp kitchen. Out in the town proper, existence was hardly more exciting – old men loitering round the doors of the betting shops and the grim little pubs; youths with black leather jackets leaning against their motorbikes with expressions of malign lassitude on their faces; snobbish women having coffee together in 'The Bay Tree' or 'The Copper Kettle'; red-faced men in tweed suits waxing pompous over drinks in the cheerless bar of the 'Tanbury Arms' . . . 'Important?' he queried aloud, 'in what way? Apart from being *my* native town?' he added with a jaunty chuckle.

That was the sort of remark that girls had always liked him for (though Cynthia had later told him they didn't; they, in fact, thought them silly, adolescent). He fastened the gaze of his very blue eyes upon her – she would like *that*, anyway. Maybe, he thought, I've been a bit unfaithful to Tanbury. He thought of its old golden-stone buildings and market square, its parish church with a tower crowned by a copper cupola, and of the hills – foothills of the Cotswolds – gently rising above it all. Pity that today the rain would all but conceal these from him!

'Oh, but you surely know,' the girl's smile suggested some special relationship she enjoyed with the truth of matters, 'that Tanbury's right there, bang in the middle of the map of British industry now? Just as it's bang in the middle of the map of England itself. Its products go out north, east, south and west, not only all over *our* country, but over Europe and beyond.'

'Really!' said James. There seemed to be no other possible response. He knew of two or three firms in the town – from all of which, doubtless, he'd been sacked at one time or another – but he had been quite unaware of Tanbury's industrial status. How very white and strong and regular this girl's teeth were, he thought; he would so like them to bite his neck and shoulders.

'I expect,' said the girl, 'that the name of Bright and Thompson will not exactly be unknown to you.'

Bright and Thompson, Bright and Thompson? Was that the

firm who had erected such a hideous complex just where the town
petered out into water-meadows by the willow-lined Grand Union
Canal and the sluggish little river Tane? The firm who had driven
Pappa to write a letter of complaint to the paper, one which had
been – most unusually – actually published: 'As a man of Oxfordshire,' Pappa had said, 'I must indignantly protest in righteous
anger against this latest temple to Mammon raised above the green
and pleasant meadows that line our town's waters' . . . 'Bright and
Thompson. Sure I know them!' James said.

'Their kitchenware's a household name, of course,' said the girl.
(Why 'of course,' wondered James.) 'Tureens, non-stick frying
pans, casserole dishes – why, even *France*, the most famous country in the whole world for such things, buys Bright and Thompson
products, you know.' After all this it was not astonishing to hear
the girl add: 'My husband Barry's the co-ordinator of the Bright
and Thompson Home Sales team, you see. And I'm the secretary
to the Accounts Department.'

'What interesting jobs!' said James, as pleasantly as he could
manage. Her words had brought into his mind those periods of his
life – in England and in America – when he too had been a member
of a Home Sales team. Years with as much value as screwed-up
pieces of paper! How, he now asked himself, had *he* sounded when
he'd sung – as he'd had to – the praises of the products of his company? (When he'd been longing to sing, all day, so very differently,
through plucked or twanged strings, or through the breathy undulations of his harmonica!) Had the bored look in his eyes always
betrayed the mechanical enthusiasms of his tongue?

Cynthia – whom he never would or could see again – had not
felt as he did about the firm for which they'd both worked. (But
then she was connected to it through her family.) Once on a steamy
Nashville evening – the fireflies were now jabbing the thick, sweet-
smelling darkness in his memory – he had jeered for almost an
hour at Vansteppen Products: 'The Donut that Does!' Cynthia had
broken a plate over his head in hurt anger, and even the ardour of
his love-making two hours later hadn't quite changed her mood.

'And what, may I ask, is taking *you* to Tanbury?'

Now, what should I say here? James asked himself. He *could* say,
could he not? that he was going to give a guitar recital (Bluegrass

and Cajun) in Tanbury Town Hall. Or that he was concerned with
the opening of a museum to commemorate his father, the distinguished writer, Hampton Varney, who had despised the commercial and had celebrated the Life-Force, the 'movement' of Nature.
But in the end he said the truth: 'I'm going to stay with old friends
there.'

'Nice!' exclaimed the girl, 'staying with old friends is always
nice, isn't it?'

It would be hard, and ungrateful too, to dispute this, and
certainly niceness was a dominant, an all-pervading characteristic
of funny old Father Lalland and his sister Frances. How good, how
constant they both had been during his time in Bencroft. But in all
honesty he wasn't really looking forward to going to their house.
How could he be? How could he feel anything but despondent
and tense today? His thirty-sixth birthday, and he had no home
in the world, in the whole vast, doomed world. His parents were
both dead and his family house (to call it by a grand and inappropriate name) sold; his wife (as he still often thought of Cynthia)
was married to another man, and he had, of course, no job nor any
prospect of one that could bring him income enough to buy for
himself even the smallest flat in Tanbury. True, there was Dan, and
Dan's place in London – Dan, his one-time idol, his adored older
brother. But for almost a year, he had found seeing him appall-
ingly trying. Talking to his brother usually made him go giddy, feel
as if his eyes would melt away, and his head dissolve. James had
not even told Dan that he was coming out of Bencroft. Dr. Stott
had applauded this, had thought it best that he kept away from his
brother for a bit and took up instead Father Lalland's many-times-
given offer of going to stay in his Vicarage.

Father Lalland had been Pappa's greatest friend, perhaps
indeed, for the better part of his life, his *only* friend. Ideologically,
one presumed, Hampton Varney and the Anglo-Catholic Vicar of
St. Jude's had little in common, Pappa having in his youth rejected
orthodox religion to worship (or so he said) the powers that
moved the sap, that drove forth the streams and rivers and caused
the four winds to blow. But socially, psychologically, well, there
they were, in a philistine country market-town, two lonely, frus-
trated, imagination-dominated men. Dan and himself had often

chuckled at the two of them, had often mocked the priest with the ungainly walk and the fat face in which the cheeks seemed to be being moved by a pair of invisible bellows. James had never thought that the day would come when this man would provide him with his only shelter against the hostile elements of life . . .

'And what, if I might be so bold as to ask, do you do?' asked the girl. James had, with Dr. Stott's aid, tried to prepare himself time and time again for such questions: they were unavoidable, he knew. Even so, he felt the saliva leave his mouth like a sudden retreat of a wave on a beach, felt a cruel knocking at his temples and a vice-like grip upon his neck – and all this within a matter of seconds.

And then James remembered his old self, that laddish James of long-receded years, famous for his ripostes and flirtations. 'I'm going to be "so bold as to ask" *you* a question,' he said, 'what do you *think* I do?' Girls' interests had often in the past been aroused in this way, though of course his reply had often also been a convenient way of evading admission that he hadn't a decent job, frequently indeed hadn't a job at all. Just as he hadn't today!

'Well,' said the girl, proffering him an orange from her bag (James declined the hateful symbol with a shake of the head), 'just give me a moment or two.' Her green-brown eyes scanned James's face. And what will she come up with? James wondered. His face and figure were still youthful, he had no surplus flesh anywhere, and his eyes, he was convinced, had lost none of their blue charm. How slowly this train is moving, he complained to himself, as the girl studied his head for her answer. It seems to be having to push itself against the wind and rain, to churn a way through these muddy fields.

'You've got the determined eyes and jaw of a man in business,' the girl said at last, 'yes, you could easily be a successful business man.' Oh, not half, thought James; he'd never for more than a few months been able to earn so much as a regular wage! 'But then you're not dressed quite like I imagine an executive would be, even for a train on Sundays.' James was wearing a new pair of jeans and a new, white polo-neck sweater; new clothes for a new life in a cleansed world. 'You also strike me as a pretty gentle sort of person.' Bang on the nail again, James thought bitterly; before his eyes appeared his own, almost luminous, fist and streaming blood and a loosened tooth and an eye closed over with swollen blue-black flesh, and then came voices whispering to him about desirable doses of bromide and shock treatment. 'No, I don't think I can put you down quite as the hardened tycoon. I've got it!' Her kittenish eyes gleamed in sudden triumph. 'You're a doctor. Yes, I'm sure of it – sensible, determined, easy-going in the way you deal with people, the kind who never loses his cool.'

I think she probably *must* fancy me to be able to produce so much sheer drivel, thought James. (Yet she would be loyal to Barry. Loyalty! Perhaps he'd been loyal only to 'The Cedars' and Blue-grass.) But a *doctor!* He wanted to laugh and laugh, to roll about on the dusty, maroon upholstery of the compartment, to tumble on the dirty floor kicking like an infant in uncontrolled mirth. What would Dr. Stott have to say to that? Or – more interesting still – Dan? Oh, of course, Dan would be very kind in his reply; he was always so dreadfully kind in all his dealings with people. 'Yes, you'd have made a good doctor, Jamesie,' he'd say, his tense, however, emphatically past conditional . . .

'Now am I right?' The girl was looking as delighted as she presumably did when the accounts department revealed the huge profits made by the sales of casserole dishes and nonstick frying pans to France. But at that moment an interruption occurred: 'Tickets, please!' said a loud, austere voice, and in the doorway of their compartment a uniformed man appeared. He was probably a bit younger than James himself – whom he resembled a little; lean body, fair hair, blue eyes – but in mien he might have belonged to another generation altogether, or perhaps to another breed of man who had but to utter and to shoot a glance to be honoured and obeyed. I'd like to tweak his stupid, bright jacket-buttons off, thought James. The man was examining the two tickets given him, as if they were brain X-rays. Which of course certain uniformed authority *had* the power to examine. In order to decide precisely what cruel wires should be put over your head; in order to probe, to reduce, to change. (It had been before the hour of the application of wires that James had seen the world as that shrinking, smelly orange about to be dropped into the void.) Imagine this stern, fair bloke before him now giving such orders: 'Yes, stronger currents into Mr. Varney's head, please. No, *still* not strong enough . . .'

'They're okay,' the B.R. official pronounced, a little grudgingly, as if there could have been real doubt about this. He moved on down the corridor. And, as if in recognition of the proven legality of the passengers, the train began to pick up speed. And nearer Tanbury, the rain fell less densely, the distinction between brown-coloured, cloudy sky and brown-coloured, muddy land became sharper – and the so familiar sequence of fields and copses and seasoned brick farmhouses, of abrupt broach-spired churches and humped bridges and serpentine streams grew easier to make out and silently to greet.

The girl gave James a conspiratorial smile as she put her ticket back into her handbag. 'Now, *come on*, now; I want to know if I was right or not,' she said, 'it's very naughty of you not to tell me. You *are* a doctor, aren't you?'

How effortless it would be for him not only to say 'Yes,' but to embellish upon the affirmative. He knew enough about doctors in all truth! But . . . 'Afraid not,' he said. *His* smile at *her* must also have been conspiratorial. James couldn't help himself now. He said: 'I'd better make a clean breast of it, hadn't I? I'm a lunatic.'

'A lunatic!' the girl's voice was almost a squeak. She gave an interrogative, anxious, but diffidently trusting laugh.

'How inaccurate I can be sometimes,' drawled James, 'what I should have said was: "*Yesterday* I was a lunatic. *Today* I'm on the lookout for an alternative occupation."'

Once again the girl's eyes explored his face. Then James saw it all: she realised that he *was* speaking – allowing for a certain melo-drama in presentation – the truth. So what was she going to say, to do? Was she perhaps going to run down the corridor in search of the ticket-collector, to clasp him saying, Authority help me! In the ensuing pause James listened to the wheels turning (burra-wurra, burra-wurra), to the rain still spattering on the carriage roof and to, in a far compartment, a transistor issuing tinkly country rock. (Memories of Nashville!) Then the girl presented to him a new smile, indeed a new facial expression, one straight out of a cosmetics advertisement: 'Oh, you men!' she said, 'you must have a very low opinion of us girls, the taradiddles you tell us and expect us to believe.' A few minutes later she was diving again into that plastic bag, and fishing out the *Bright and Thompson House Magazine*. She read it all the way to Tanbury, and really who could blame her? James felt ashamed. She had been friendly, interested, kind. And he, he was perhaps no longer capable of being any of those things. Better if he could have led the life of an unhampered wild animal.

James had visited Tanbury only once in the past eighteen months, in order to – but he must *not* recall that day. Whenever he'd imagined coming back to the town, he'd pictured the sun shining down upon its streets and the surrounding country. But perhaps today's wet weather was more appropriate to the occasion. Wetness imposed resignation and James had little enough reason to adopt any attitude but this to Fate. But resignation had never come easily to him. He had to make a conscious effort not to turn left at the end of the station yard, the direction he would have taken to get to 'The Cedars', today, of course, in other hands. (But whose? Dan, who'd sold it, must have told him.) Instead James now walked over the canal bridge, and up a street, lined with drab late 19th-century terrace houses but from which fields were visible, towards St. Jude's Church and Vicarage. There they stood, Victorian church and the rambling house he'd been invited, indeed requested, to think of as his home. Through veils of grey rain they awaited him. Him, the black and lunatic sheep who'd gone astray and over whose return there would be more rejoicing in Heaven than there ever would be over Dan, whose life had been so sensible, busy and blameless.

6

Three lunches – two in Madrid (eaten separately), one in Oxfordshire – during which each person thought wonderingly about the other two.

After two steamy, lecherous hours in the sauna, Kevin had taken himself to a somewhat scruffy café-bar near the Chueca metro. Out of its windows and open door he could watch some small boys vigorously kicking a football about the dusty square; he would willingly, he felt, accept the gift of transformation into one of them. Weren't they living life as it should be lived? He ate economically; a large tortilla sandwich, and a glass of Mahou beer. Presently he was joined by his pals, Nolo and Paco. Both – eyes glittering and hands energetic in narrative gestures – had a lot to tell about adventures last night. Nolo had fetched up in a luxurious flat in the Calle de Velázquez belonging to two antique dealers who'd wanted from him the strangest gratifications.

Sometime, Kevin thought, I must go back to my drawings. A few sketches of Marilyn Monroe, done at Nolo's instigation, aren't enough. I liked the imaginary animals I drew, making up to lonely youths, my portraits of Theo and the man in Marseilles and – damn him! – of Jason; I liked my design for an ideal room; with a bed like a huge luxuriant bird's nest, and leaves painted (or perhaps, stuck) on to the wall, and bookshelves and receptacles for clothes and cosmetics placed on bough-like structures. A year ago I'd busy myself with such things. But a year ago, he continued to himself, I didn't guess that I would be leading this strange but demanding life in Madrid – indeed I'd never thought about Madrid except as a frequent name in Daddy's conversation. This time last year had been the worst day of his life – that unforgettable look of agony, that attempt at violence, then those unseeing eyes! It had been the day too, of course, on which he had been given the harmonica.

Lunch that Sunday last November was obscured for him by these other, more sombre memories. Presumably he'd eaten it at Uncle Edward's Vicarage, and, Aunt Frances having cooked it, it would have consisted of tasty, traditional English dishes. Kevin could not know, that, at the very moment he was thinking about him, James was in the setting in his mind, seated at the Lallands' dining-table, hoping that, wrought-up though he was, he'd be able to do justice to what was no doubt going to be a hearty meal.

Outside the Vicarage windows he could see the rain dripping via the bare branches of the crab-apple tree onto the lawn. Within, nicely emphasising the chill of the weather without, a log-fire burned in the fireplace. Before they started eating, Father Lalland mumbled for an amazingly long time a grace in Latin ('a favourite grace of dear Father Tapham-Thompson – R.I.P. – of my old joint, the Community of the Resurrection at Mirfield'), a grace that eventually came to an end with the words: 'And now, my dear boy, tuck in.' And tuck in they all indeed did – into duck served with cherries and a cherry-and-orange sauce, roast potatoes, swedes and Brussels sprouts, and afterwards a pretty, buoyantly light Queen of Puddings over which they poured thick, fresh cream. It was a delicious lunch but – it's odd to think of me sitting here eating it, said James to himself, me who wanted the world of freedom, and ardent sexual love, long, dusty, open roads, shared rides through unknown country and visits to whorehouses . . .

'It's a very old English practice, serving duck with cherries,' Frances Lalland was saying, 'and one not sufficiently known about. Funnily enough I came across a reference to it in a short story by Mrs. Gaskell, only the other day. I can't remember the exact words but the passage went something like: "It was Thursday, and the Vicar was coming round for dinner that evening, so *roast duck with cherries* was decided upon."'

I wonder if the rest of the story was equally thrilling, thought James. He composed his features into a smile of boyish gratitude for good grub while Father Lalland made a verbal reply to his sister's remarks. 'I can tell you *one* vicar who would have been *very* pleased if he'd gone round to the Gaskellite household for dinner that Thursday,' he said, those invisible bellows working vigorously away inside his cheeks, 'and he's not a hundred miles away!'

'It certainly all tastes very good,' James said, feeling after this that a compliment was expected of him. Frances Lalland looked pleased at his words.

'Duck with cherries seems to have enjoyed a special popularity, however, in our neighbouring Northamptonshire,' she was pleased to continue, a little relentlessly in James's opinion, 'one Women's Institute at Brackley collected up a hundred ways of eating fowl (at least I think it was one hundred; it may have been only fifty), and roast duck *in this particular style* cropped up again and again.'

'Gosh!' said James, he hoped not inappropriately, realising that Frances Lalland probably found it as hard to think of things to say to him as he did to her, 'well, they're a sensible county if duck cooked that way always tastes like this.'

'Eating fowl!' exclaimed Father Lalland wheezily, 'a sad, sad thought when you muse upon it. I wouldn't ever have wanted to

eat any of our Baggy Trousered Chickens, would you, Frances?'
These, James recalled, were a curious species of hen with legs all
covered by a sort of fur, which the Lallands had long kept. 'How
lucky that they really weren't and aren't good for the pot. It's really
for the interestingness of their company that one keeps Baggy
Trousered Chickens, don't you think?'

James felt incompetent to reply to this. He accepted a refill of
his glass – Father Lalland had provided a sweet, nutty German
white wine – and then said: 'The room you've put me in is *Kevin's*,
isn't it? How *is* the lad these days?' His tone was his heartiest, but
maybe it didn't really conceal the tension he was feeling. Nervily
he jigged his leg underneath the table and watched how shadows
now stole across the pale blue eyes of both Edward and Frances
Lalland.

'Didn't he, hasn't he written to you at all, while you were in
Bencroft?' said the latter, her voice quietly begging James to give
an affirmative reply.

'Well,' said James, 'of course he may have done at the beginning: I hardly took in any of the letters I got then, as you know,
and I also threw them away pretty easily, often unread. But after
the first month, I don't think he did.'

And why *should* he? James asked himself; we weren't that intimate. Indeed his recollections of the boy were dim; though hadn't
they shared some rich experiences? But he could not remember
what these were.

'Dear James,' said Father Lalland, 'how fond Kevin became of
you when he was staying here, and you were still living at "The
Cedars". You gave him so much pleasure and he – yes, I would say
he looked up to you, as I never knew him to do to anybody else.
Wouldn't you agree, Frances?'

'Indeed I would!' said Frances Lalland, intensely, laying down
her knife and fork in a gesture that made James feel almost afraid,
'indeed I would!'

James felt as if he were Lazarus resurrected (well, perhaps his
condition wasn't so very different), but a Lazarus hazy about the
life to which he'd come back. 'In what way did I give him pleasure?' he asked, not fishing for compliments, merely desirous of
information. 'Can't imagine what I could give to anyone, least of

all to a kid on the threshold of life – me, an out-of-work hobo who's failed on two continents.'

Frances Lalland cut into this: 'You *must* stop talking like that about yourself, James, you really must. You've been good to *many* people, and our nephew Kevin was not the least of them. You ask us what you did to give him pleasure. A lot – is my reply. How many other men in their thirties would have bothered to play tunes, even to sing, to someone scarcely out of his adolescence, to explain to him the working of the instruments, to . . . ?'

'Oh, I'd bore anyone with my *music*,' James said, laughing a little in self-derision. 'If you gave me half a chance, I'd even stop eating this excellent duck and rush upstairs now for my guitar. (Don't worry, I'm not going to!) But you can't call *that* "good" of me. You ought to have heard my ex-wife, Cynthia, on the subject of me and my musical instruments!'

'We *can* call it good of you,' Frances Lalland reprimanded him, with a tranquil severity, 'and, to continue: you took him badger-watching in Foxton Woods.'

'Yes, yes,' said James, nodding at this, as if he and Kevin had suddenly appeared in a moving picture on the wall opposite, pushing their way through ferns and willowherb towards the setts and the stream. 'Yes, I did do that. At least I *think* I did.' But more vivid was another, solitary visit to Foxton Woods paid during the same period.

'And before you left Tanbury,' Frances Lalland said, 'you gave him your harmonica!'

So that's where it had gone to. He had forgotten. And yet now he did perhaps – if only faintly – recall the November day, with vapours rising from piles of dead leaves and wrapping themselves round the trunks of trees, when he'd said to Kevin: 'Kiddo, *you* have this. I reckon I won't be needing it now.' It had been the same day as . . .

'I gave him my harmonica,' he repeated aloud. But *why* exactly? he asked himself. Presumably something in Kevin Lalland had touched him, though he could give it no name today. 'But you still haven't answered my question,' he said, accepting Miss Lalland's offer of more potatoes, more Brussels sprouts, 'what is Kevin doing now?'

'We're not sure exactly,' said Frances Lalland, with obvious discomfort, 'but we've good reason to believe he's still in Spain, haven't we, Edward?'

'Yes, in Spain,' her brother puffed in agreement, 'in Sunny Spain – and it wouldn't be difficult for Spain to be a *little* sunnier than Tanbury, Oxon, would it now? "Rain, rain, go to Spain" that's what I say!' And he pretended to shake a fist at the weather outside the window.

'But *why* has Kevin gone to Spain?' James persisted. Somehow he couldn't imagine him living abroad. Those gentle ways had surely been so extremely English.

'It's so hard to say why, so hard to speak about it all,' Frances Lalland answered, a little pleadingly. 'There were grave difficulties with his parents.' (Aren't there always? said James to himself.) 'Gerald and Christina – well, fond as we are of them, both Edward and I feel that they lack understanding in important areas. They have *never* fully appreciated Kevin's great sensitivity. So you see, when Kevin had that decisive quarrel with his boss, they, oh, dear, it *is* all so *very* hard!! *You* must understand that, of all people.'

'Are you implying that *I* had something to do with it all?' asked James, deducing this from Miss Lalland's hesitations and eye-play rather than from her words, though through the stressed pronoun in the last sentence had sounded a gentle note of accusation.

'Oh, James, you've got so much time at your disposal here,' Frances Lalland said. This time her tone was not so much pleading as informed by a certain prohibitive quality. 'Let's go into the matter another time. Not during your *first lunch* here.'

Well, I suppose I *do* owe it to them not to probe, not to make them feel emotional disquietude, James said to himself. But I don't understand all this at all.

'Not during your *first lunch*, no!' Father Lalland reproduced but a little more emphatically his sister's rhythms, 'and what a very good lunch it is too! Personally I feel quite ready for a little more of the roast quack-quack. How about anyone else?'

On the walls of the café where Dan was having lunch, posters displayed leading bullfighters in gaudy, defiant, ritual attitudes upon rose or yellow backgrounds. Its floor – a gleaming, clean marble – was profusely strewn with empty cigarette packets, torn paper napkins and crumpled sugar-lump wrappers; and by the fruit-machines, which pinged out with irksome frequency the Harry Lime theme, eager clusters of noisy, good-humoured youths were standing. Outside the café the Rastro! He was having to force himself to eat and drink. He had slept but little after his discovery of the harmonica in its black case; questions had been as flies buzzing round a dead limpet. *How* had Kevin met James? Where? Why had James given him the instrument he loved so dearly? Did Kevin know James's present fate?

And now of course Kevin's remarks in the Paseo last night came back to Dan – though never, for a minute, had he suspected that his brother was their subject: '*I love the harmonica for itself, and I love it for its personal associations. It was a present from someone who means – no, meant, no, means – a lot to me.*' Didn't those confusions in tenses suggest that Kevin knew what had happened to James? Kevin had also said: '*For one minute I thought you were that someone who gave me the Hohner*' . . . So considerable, for all their earlier closeness, had been their differences in adult life, that Dan had often found himself thinking about James and himself as if they were not brothers. As Kevin – not knowing what he was speaking of – had gone on to remark, their complexions, builds, features were unalike. But brothers they were, and, somewhere in their psyches, manifesting themselves externally from time to time, there must be elements peculiar to the two of them.

But . . . outside the café window, outside the window of his perplexed mind, was the Rastro.

The porter at his hotel had recommended to Dan as antidotes to the Franquista demonstrations – the morning's preparations for which had been as disturbing as last night's activities in the Paseo roadway – first the church of San Antonio de la Florida, and then this: Madrid's huge Sunday market. What contrasts! In the overwhelming peace of the monastery church Dan had experienced – possibly as a result of his mental turmoil of the night and early morning – a sensation so unexpected and vivid that – well, he didn't want to think about it just yet. The Rastro, on the other hand, could offer no such numinous moment, it was all people and pell-mell objects, so many people and so many objects upon pave-

ment and stalls that progress along its sequence of old streets and
little squares had been exceedingly slow, and the view of the bare,
brown undulations to the south of the city was frequently blotted
out.

What did the Rastro not have to sell! Charming bowls with
traditional patterns, hideous bowls with coy cats' faces luminously
painted on them, jeans and T-shirts, old *mantones de mantilla* which
you could not believe in anyone wearing, birds of brilliant hue
shut up in obscenely small cages, chests and barrels containing –
nothing. Dan felt no desire to buy anything – who would he buy
things for, anyway? James would reject a birthday present! – and,
during his examinations of the stalls, he found himself thinking
obsessively about where the many curious possessions of his
father had ended up – for after his death Dan had sold them all.
The signed photograph of Knut Hamsun, the paintings by Friedrich Mayerhofer, the bust of Goethe, the splinter of wood from
Shakespeare's cradle – would one day he encounter these in such a
place as Madrid's Rastro? Would people be exclaiming over them:
'Whoever could have wanted *these*? I can't envisage a household
in which they would be in place, can you?' And yet objects fascinated, delighted, even in their abandoned solitudes. A coffee-pot
lid, a cracked plate separated from its fellows, a huge gilded cage
with no provisions for a bird, these spoke for themselves, as the
attention of eyes and hands were, at this minute, demonstrating.
And why not? *Why*, Dan asked himself, this mania for wholeness
by which we are all possessed? The whole as an *Ideal* by whose
light we appreciate the fragmented, that's how it should be. He
thought, as he brought the Rastro's *bric-à-brac* back to his eyes, of
Kevin – not living in any recognised whole, by dint of his sexuality:
he thought too of patients choking out bits and pieces of words or
phrases. *Wholeness!*

Dan had a meal similar to Kevin's – a *tortilla*, though not
encased in a sandwich, *Mahou* beer, and a Viennese pastry stuffed
with marzipan. At the table next to him a young couple – their
eyes often meeting in new fondness – were obviously discussing
an article in the Sunday edition of *El Pais*. Its colour supplement
lay open before them on the table's formica top. Somehow Dan
associated colour supplements entirely with his own society. Was

it possible, for instance, that the boy and girl near him could be reading an article comparable to that he himself had read a year ago, an article which had broken up 'The Cedars' more effectively than any subsequent sale of its effects?

Even now Dan found it difficult to accept that Jason Fletcher had written the piece (and where *had* his intimate-seeming knowledge of Pappa come from?). Jason . . . maybe one day he would bring himself to meet his old friend again (Jason had proposed meetings) and discover the reason, the real reason that was, behind his splashing of verbal vitriol.

From the day of his arrival, lively and bright-eyed, at Tanbury Grammar School, Jason had made an impact on Dan that went far beyond merely wanting his company or wondering what he thought about such-and-such a thing. His combination of mocking self-sufficiency and of mocking desire for regard had made him a magnetic figure for both Richard Cardew and himself – and maybe, for a short baleful period, for James.

From the first, Jason had displayed the keenest curiosity about Dan's father. 'He's a writer by *profession*, you say?'

'Right!' For never would either James or himself admit to the outside world that they were supported not by Pappa's books (all long out of print) but by a combination of his dwindling 'competence' and Mamma's earnings as secretary to Stephen Thomas, the area's leading solicitor.

'Does he contribute to any magazine or newspaper in particular?'

'Not nowadays,' said Dan, 'but at one time he wrote a great deal for *The European*.'

'Never-'eard-of-it!' said Jason, and indeed well might he not! 'It's scarcely on every station bookstall, is it?'

'You see,' Dan said, ignoring this, 'Pappa prefers to reserve his energy these days for his creative work.' He could hear something of Hampton Varney's pomposity in his own tone.

'So that's what *Pappa* prefers, is it?' said Jason, 'and when did *Pappa*'s last book come out?'

'I'm not sure of the exact date,' lied Dan.

'A long time ago?'

'Quite a long time ago. But he's working on a new book now.'

'Really. What about?'

'Shakespeare,' said Dan reluctantly, and knowing himself to be blushing.

'Well, *there's* a novel subject,' said Jason, 'I wonder how he came to think of it! Don't you think it funny that no books of his are in my dad's library?' (The County Library.) 'I'd like to know why they aren't. Distinguished local author and all . . .'

Jason and his interest in Pappa – his malicious interest! To what dreadful events it had led. First to the fight in the cricket pavilion with James. And lastly to the article of last year – so like in format to what the couple at the next table were animatedly talking over. 'A Sort of Phoenix' had been its title.

A Phoenix that had ascended only inches in the air to turn to the ashes from which it had risen . . .

The Harry Lime theme pinged out yet again from the fruit machine, Zarzuela music proceeded from a corner radio, the couple at the next table now laughed at a common joke. Sometimes, Dan said to himself, the only city I want to visit is one situated by the River Lethe. To bathe in oblivion of the past would be a sweet, sweet experience for me.

And then the whole matter of Kevin, his possession of James's harmonica, and his disappearance resurrected itself. To endure in his head for the whole afternoon.

He found himself longing for the arrival of Richard Cardew that night.

7

The Lallands made little attempt to disguise their anxiety when James announced after lunch that he'd like to go for a walk by himself. You could watch them striving for the best way of preventing him: was it really wise to set out in such weather? He'd probably get soaked to the skin! Where was he thinking of walking to, anyway?

'Oh, I'd just like to stroll into Tanbury proper and take a look at the old place again,' James said jauntily, 'it'd be interesting to see whether any of my old haunts have changed while I've been away from them.'

The priest and his sister exchanged worried glances. Clearly the references both to haunts and to his absence from these disconcerted them. Christ, will I have to endure this palaver *every* time I want to leave the bloody house? James asked himself. It's good of them to be so concerned about me, of course, but . . . 'At Bencroft,' he said, 'they always encouraged me to take as much exercise as I could, and I went for lots of solitary rambles.' But not through scenes of former emotional pain, the Lallands' faces replied. But they could not bring themselves to articulate this in words, and so just before four o'clock James left the Vicarage, promising, however, to be back within an hour and a half.

It felt strange to be approaching the centre of Tanbury from the south-east – where was situated St. Jude's – rather than from the north-west, compass-point of 'The Cedars'. It was a bit like playing in a looking-glass version of your life. The colourlessness of the sky and the fact of its being Sunday had divested Tanbury of almost all its individuality. The grey clouds amassed in the sky diminished that landmark, the lofty, greeny-gold cupola on top of the 17th-century parish church; the honey-coloured stone of the older buildings of the town did not glow as it usually did. The bare chestnut trees that graced the town's most distinguished street, the Horse Fair, looked sorry rather than noble, all webbed with rain. While as for the less distinguished streets, with their red-brick Victorian buildings and their bleak entrances to now empty shopping arcades, they could have been encountered in a hundred featureless Midlands towns. Even allowing for the weather and the day, James was surprised at how deserted the town was. Back in Bencroft, that sequestered establishment standing in its own park, Tanbury had always remained bustling and populous in his mental pictures. This afternoon the place resembled some townscape in a disagreeable dream. All pubs and cafés were closed, of course, and shop windows were lightless blank eyes. In the Horse Fair, clustered round their wet motorbikes, and standing by the entrance to the horribly pretty Cotswold-style public lavatories, were groups of black-leather-jacketed youths. 'Sid Vicious Was Right!' read the slogan on one youth's back (right about what? James wondered), while another ran: 'Bastards Unite!' But haven't they done so already? James asked himself. At any rate against *me*. His life

seemed to have been full of them – Mr. Denistone and Mr. Dawes
at school who'd jeered at him for being, as they thought, stupid
and lazy; Pappa, who'd tended to treat his second son as if he had
no responsibility for his making; all those would-be members of
the Establishment who'd sacked him from jobs, really all because
he refused to lick their arses; Jason Fletcher – supremely, of course;
even at times Dan, with his contained, over-rational ways.

James continued past 'The Market Cross' and 'The Pig and
Whistle'. From the first he'd been chucked out on several occasions for being too drunk (it was a snooty place); the second,
however, had been the scene of musical triumphs – if limited ones.
And now past J. Higgins, Newsagent . . . James, in his enterprising
adolescence, had, much to his mother's disapproval, done a paper
round for Mr. Higgins in order to earn the money with which to
buy or repair musical instruments. There were some in Tanbury
who pronounced Mr. Higgins to be a self-righteous windbag, but
James, who would surely have been the first to take exception to
such a person, had always liked the old boy. He was the sort who
didn't care what others thought about his opinions. Indeed a real
affection had grown up between the two of them, Mr. Higgins
always – rather touchingly – taking an interest in James's musical
activities and (as they both tried to see them) achievements:
performances at a pub, at a dance. Six months ago he had attended
Pappa's funeral, and James had been very glad to see him there
in the church, in his cheap black suit, his slightly misshapen face
wearing a thoughtful, compassionate expression. But he hadn't
managed to speak to him, indeed wouldn't have been capable of
doing so, in such a state had he been, out on 'parole', as it were,
from Bencroft.

Stopping before the window of his old employer's shop, James
saw propped up against guidebooks to the Cotswolds and Oxfordshire the latest edition of the *Tanbury Echo*. (He had last looked
at the local newspaper on the occasion of his father's death:
'Suddenly from a heart-attack. Once thought to be a writer of
promise . . . Controversial political interests, earning him a great
deal of later difficulties . . . Deep feeling for the Tanbury area . . .
Indisputably a man of Oxfordshire, though, and proud to be so.')
Today the paper's headlines importantly proclaimed: PLANS FOR

NEW SWIMMING BATH APPROVED AT LAST. Well! . . . really swimming *was* as important as most other things, thought James. Life was probably only to be borne when you concentrated on the pleasures of a bathe, of a drink, of a tune played or listened to. (His harmonica – given away to that boy whom he could remember so little.)

And now Tanbury's famous Cross reared itself before him. It was a replete Victorian monument, built on the site of the medieval one which had given rise to the well-known old nursery rhyme:

> 'Ride-a-cock horse to
> Tanbury Cross
> To see a fine lady
> upon a white horse.
> Rings on her fingers
> and bells on her toes.
> She shall have music
> wherever she goes.'

So – swimming, modest drinking, music . . . was it therefore such people as the planners of town baths that you should be admiring? James tried to envisage them. No, he couldn't see them as passionately concerned with enabling men, women and children to obtain a release from care through experiences of the element of water; rather he saw them as the fat, stuffy fathers of the less acceptable of his former schoolmates. (Which is precisely what some of them would be.) The kind of men, in other words, who'd treated Pappa as a pariah, who refused to see the nobility of the man. Bastards! Pappa too, of course, had been a bastard – at any rate to James. But these men's 'bastardy' was, he was sure, worse. Interested only in their position and in how much money they could cram into their pockets. Pappa had surely been right in his unstinting condemnation of the mercantile world – James had learned *that* lesson in Nashville. Right in his belief that instead of the 'breeding of money upon money' there should be the surrender to the call of the sap, of the rivers, of the many motions of wind and sky. But just how did one do this – without plunging into chaos? Had Pappa surrendered himself – in the way he advocated in his books and talk? What about poor, pretty, bewildered but proud Mamma slaving away at an uncongenial job in an office, to keep them all afloat?

In this afternoon's sky heaved clouds, pregnant with more and imminent rain. The Lallands would soon be vindicated; he'd be soaked to the skin, that somehow appetising phrase. Now he was passing the sash-windowed front of Dr. Cardew's surgery. Dr. Cardew who'd examined him for syphilis which he thought he'd caught off some hippy girl encountered when she was selling flowers on Victoria Station, Dr. Cardew who, on his return from Nashville, had helped him over his drinking problem, Dr. Cardew who finally – presumably in collusion with Dan – had recommended that he go to Bencroft. And Dr. Cardew who was, of course, the father of brother Dan's oldest friend, Richard.

James saw Richard before him now; thin, pale face with spectacles, tousled hair, dirty hands, and clothes that always seemed crumpled and unkempt. James had always liked the bloke, though they had had little in common: Richard had invented a language when he was younger ('Bonalingus') which Dan had been able to learn, but James, needless to say, had not; later Richard had specialised in languages. Very close since the age of eight, Richard and Dan had nevertheless admitted into their company Jason Fletcher when he arrived, so full of himself, in the Sixth Form of the Grammar School. Jason with his intellectual airs and swagger, and almost permanent derisive smile, was just the kind of guy who got on James's wick. 'In many ways I'm like Henrik Ibsen,' he'd said, 'my ambition is to set the torpedo under the ark of society.' A torpedo under his own arse would have been more to the point. The crud was only the son of the local librarian, not of a proper writer and philosopher like Pappa, and he lived in a dreadful little 'cornflake-packet' house up in the Meadowborough Estate. And yet he could sneer at Pappa, ask snide question after snide question, and eventually make terrible accusations. James never could forget that May afternoon (it had been Dan's seventeenth birthday) for long. Even now, as his letter to him had indicated, he rejoiced in the impact of his own hard fists on Jason's soft flesh. Take that, you bastard! and *that*, and *that*!

Yet who had the victory now – Jason, writing ever more lucrative and fame-bringing articles for leading papers, or himself, a nobody with an unsound mind?

All the time he'd been tramping the length of the Horse Fair he had known what his destination would be. Not 'The Cedars' today; he wasn't quite ready for his old home yet. (He bet the present owner didn't tend it like he'd done.) 'The Cedars' would remind him of past miseries, yes, but also of a past security. The place he was bound for defied thoughts of past and future.

He turned to his right, into a road which climbed quite gently up a hillside and was bordered with wide grass verges. And now the raindrops began to fall once more, though slowly. Copsestock Road was, in point of fact, the quickest way to the open country from the centre of Tanbury, but it was not to the country that James was now going. Rather to the frontier of another kind of country.

James had forgotten how big the cemetery was. The declining light, the increasing rain made its far walls seem strangely distant from the wrought-iron gates of the entrance. He looked about him to get his bearings, and, as he did so, his temples throbbed, rods seemed to be being twisted behind his eyes and his neck held in a vice-like grip. Steady on, he told himself, steady on – *I'm thirty-six years old today, remember!* (And who would know *that* better than those he was, so to speak, about to visit.) He forced himself up and along the straight, wet, bleak walks of the place, wondering – will *I* one day lie here, and if I do, will anyone ever come to visit *me*? Dan, he supposed, might. One thing was sure: he'd not been responsible for any child coming into the world, so there could be no son to parallel his own glum, resentful pilgrimage of today. Down the gaunt slabs and crosses that presided over the graves drops of water were coursing; as a result of the wet afternoon the flowers at the foot of them were sodden and the soil made mud.

He came upon the pair of them a little sooner than he'd expected. On his left hand, 'Olivia Varney: Beloved Wife of Hampton Varney and Mother of Daniel and James'. On his right, 'Hampton Varney'. On Pappa's almost obscenely new marble gravehead no details of his earthly relationships were recorded – perhaps just as well. Instead there glowered out in gold the quotation from the *Rig-Veda* that he'd wanted as his epitaph:

'Creep away to this broad vast earth, the mother that is kind and gentle. She is a young girl, soft as wool. She will guard you from the lap of destruction.'

What bilge, James thought, what fucking stupid bilge! Had Pappa sincerely believed such stuff? Indeed how much of all that he'd gone booming on about *had* he really believed? The earth a mother, a young girl, my arse! And even if she were, it didn't mean she'd treat you well, did it?

For only half a year had Hampton Varney lain in this spot. Before that he too had been walking up the Horse Fair, circumnavigating the Market Cross. One place however he had, in the last months of his life, *not* left Tanbury for was Bencroft. James, he'd said, was no longer to be thought of as his son. 'And I did not want to think of you as a father,' James said to the slab, 'but how could I do anything else? I didn't say so then, but *now* I can! I *hated* you.' But the verb seemed to dissolve upon the vaporous air.

It would have been good to offset his images of his father, prophet-like in appearance, adamantly hostile towards himself in expression, with ones of his mother. She'd been a handsome, fair-minded woman, golden-haired and blue-eyed like himself. But Mamma had died when he was only seventeen, over half his lifetime ago. Sometimes he found it hard to remember her at all, to believe in her ever having existed, though in the worst stages of his depressive illness her deathbed had been exceedingly vivid to him – her pretty mouth all bunged up with evil-smelling fluid, her eyeballs discoloured, her whole body ravaged by the cancer that was killing her, and Pappa, a distraught and incredulous madman, pacing the corridor outside her bedroom.

Suddenly on this rainy afternoon they both seemed to be looking at him with eyes of wind-chilled stone.

'Happy birthday,' they said to him but there was no well-wishing, let alone jubilation, detectable in their voices.

'Thank you,' said James, 'I'm . . .'

'We know,' came their voices, clear like funeral bells, 'thirty-six. Well, how do you feel, James? Older and saner, we trust, than you did yesterday.'

'Older, certainly. I *should* resent the way you're talking, but I don't. You've a right to do so; I'm nobody to be proud of. Not that either of you ever were. You both preferred Dan, and who could blame you? He was cleverer than me, wiser than me, more virtuous than me. You, Mamma, never saw me drinking, never saw me whoring, having rows, getting into money-troubles, but you somehow divined that I'd do such things one day; I could tell it, even then, from those detachedly, pleasantly contemptuous smiles you used to give me. And you, Pappa, well, of course you *did* know all about my vices, had eyewitness experience of some of them. But you weren't much bothered about what had caused me to indulge in them – after all what did the peccadilloes of an untalented son matter compared with the "twin Pole Stars" of Shakespeare and Goethe, with your own "apprehensions" of the Power behind Nature? But I suppose if you can see me at all, you'd think yourself as justified in the low opinion you always held of me. All I've been good for is to play tunes from a country you wrote off as barbarian on instruments you never cared for. (And even that, only on a private, amateur level – with my favourite instrument given away!) I turned out to be a lousy husband who drove his wife out of the house after only four months (is that a record?); I've proved totally unemployable, and totally incapable of making sound judgements or managing money. (My own, that is – I looked after *yours*, Pappa, carefully enough!) And, of course, emotionally and mentally unstable. When I was sent into Bencroft, you said that I'd betrayed the Life-Force and had entered the regions of Death. It was, of course, more convenient for you to see it that way than to realise I was unhappy beyond any bearing. But again maybe you weren't so far off the mark as all that; I certainly feel as if I'm held captive in those regions of Death, yes, even now I'm better. Feel I'm someone who could *deliver* death too – to himself, to others. Look at my hands, Mamma and Pappa, look at them, and see how suited they are to dealing destruction.'

'James Varney – it *is* James Varney, isn't it?'

James swung round. As he did so, he proved the old cliché true: his heart really did feel as if it had come into his mouth. Who could be addressing him in this deserted place? And how much of his speech to his parents had he in fact spoken aloud?

'Yes, it is. Well, good to see you, James.'

And there stood Mr. Higgins holding out to him a horny, damp, dirty hand.

'But I was thinking about you only a while back!' James exclaimed. Here, on Death's frontier, Mr Higgins' ugly, asymmetrical face with the over-noticeable carbuncle on the nose was welcome beyond words. 'I walked past your shop on the way here, you see, and it all came back to me – how nice you were to work with, how you trusted me. Nobody since then has ever been pleased to have me around the way you seemed to be.'

'The way I *was*,' corrected Mr. Higgins, 'you were a real joy to have in the shop, James, and out on the rounds too. I hope you'll forgive me for intruding upon you when you were paying your respects to your mum and dad, but I just couldn't let an opportunity of talking to you pass by. It seems such a very long time since we met; I couldn't get to speak to you at your father's funeral. But I wrote to you in Bencroft. Did you ever get my letter?'

'Mr. Higgins, I can't remember,' James said, 'I've forgotten so *many* things. But I'm very glad you've come over now to speak to me.' For paying respects is hardly the right word for what I was doing, he privately added: it's as well that I was interrupted.

'I've just been visiting my wife's auntie's grave,' Mr. Higgins was saying, 'putting some flowers on it.' (Chrysanthemums, probably, for the rain to batter into mush.) 'Miss Kendall: I wonder if you recall her? She passed over shortly after your dad did. Lived in Sandown Road and used to serve in the bakery in the Market Square. Hers was a good, long life, but that doesn't make her going any the less sad, does it? Of course, she's with Jesus now, but I like to think she can see me, honouring her last resting-place.'

'Resting-place!' said James. Such talk had always made him very shy. Because it was such twaddle, wasn't it? Just like that quotation from the *Rig-Veda*. But he mustn't mock, mustn't despise. Wasn't there something fine in the way this nice man came on wretched Sunday afternoons to honour an old fat lady whom James remembered for the little giggles with which she'd punctuated her remarks and a ludicrous taste in hats? . . . The gravestones seemed to be swaying before him in the winter afternoon miasma; there was a thrush with ruffled feathers and bright eyes, he noticed, pecking on the gravel sprinkled over Pappa's grave. The bird too began to quiver, to move up and down, up and down in rhythm with his own shoulders . . . James had been a tough lad, good for fights and rough sport, but crying – through hurt feelings – had always come painfully easily to him.

'Don't laddie, don't!' Mr. Higgins was laying a hand upon his back to steady him. 'I know it must be sad for you today to stand in this place, but there's comfort to be taken from it, you know. You may not be a believer like me (you're too young still, maybe) but I tell you – they're at peace, your mum and dad.'

'But I'm not,' James heard himself choking out, 'and I'm never going to be, Mr. Higgins, never. And it isn't as if I'm still young like you said; I'm not a "laddie" – I'm thirty-six today. And I don't want another birthday.'

'James, I've got the van outside. It's not good for you to be here any longer. Let me run you to . . . to where? The station? Are you still at Bencroft?'

'No, they let me out today. A sort of birthday present for me,' James laughed through his tears. 'I'm staying with the Lallands at St. Jude's Vicarage.'

'Ah, your father's friends!'

'That's right!' But had Father Lalland, for all his longstanding friendship with Pappa, James wondered, ever really seen what the man was like? Indeed, with his innocent enthusiasms – his special Baggy Trousered Chickens, his sister's cooking, Anglo-Catholic ritual, garden shrubs – how could he have done so?

'Well, I'll take you to the Vicarage now,' Mr. Higgins was saying, 'I would say: "Come and have some tea at our place" – I know my wife, Dorothy, would be very pleased to see you – but then we've got the grandchildren round, you see. They get a bit out of hand at times, and you might be better off without noisy company today.'

Christ, James felt tired, and weak too. He who'd been so robust, and still looked it. For two pins he wouldn't mind being back in Bencroft, hearing bells and nurses' feet sounding with assuring regularity down the over-hygienic corridors, feeling the lonely but ultimately untroubling parkland closing in upon him for the night. The slabs and crosses once more shook before his brimming eyes, the eyes of James Varney, master-Bluegrass player, seasoned drinker, good cocksman (to use a favourite phrase of his Southern

buddies, one that had occurred to him this morning when confronted by the pretty girl from Bright and Thompson).

'Creep away to this broad, vast earth, the mother that is kind
and gentle . . .'

He wished he'd never read the inscription; Dan must have seen
to its engravure. The mother that is . . . But there were things in
life that could at least *appear* kind and gentle – the soft rain, even
though it could give you chills and ruin flowers; the thrush upon
the gravel, even though it would be merciless with worms; Mr.
Higgins . . .

'I'm . . . feeling funny,' James all but cried, putting his hand to
his head. Objects in his surroundings were not merely swaying
now; they were threatening him with advances.

Mr. Higgins lent him an arm for support and together they
walked slowly out of the cemetery. There's no fucking need for
anybody to be buried anywhere, James thought. It only compounds
the cruelty of life above ground. 'You're going to be all right,' Mr.
Higgins was telling him, 'you'll always turn out all right, you know,
for all your difficulties. You must just accept that you're someone
who won't have an easy passage through this world.'

True, doubtless, but *why* shouldn't he? Why should he have to
accept so depressing a fact? Second by second the rain was falling
more densely. Once inside Mr. Higgins' van you could hear it ener-
getically pattering on the roof; Mr. Higgins turned on the windscreen wipers.

'You *thought*,' James heard himself saying, as his old boss started
up the engine, 'that I was paying my respects to my parents. But I
must tell you that I wasn't, not at all. I was telling them, as if they
could see and hear me, that I *loathed* them. Terrible, wasn't it? But
you are aware, aren't you? that when I was in Bencroft, my father
refused so much as to visit me. Even when they put wires to my
brain and administered electric shocks, he couldn't bring himself
to see the bum he'd brought into the world.'

Mr. Higgins made no direct reply to this. Then he said: 'Talked
to your brother recently? Now there's a nice man.'

'Too nice, I think,' said James sadly, 'it's not wise for Dan and me to have much to do with each other at the moment. I haven't even told him I was leaving Bencroft; I just didn't want him, you see, to be there to witness my faltering steps back into the world.' Not to mention, he privately added, all those many unspoken tensions between us. Which might get spoken! Such as – why couldn't Dan have exerted *more* influence on Pappa and *made* him come over to Bencroft? Why did Dan only notify me of Pappa's heart attack after its lethal work was over? Was it because he wanted to remain the only good son of the two of us right to the very end?

Mr. Higgins was driving down Copsestock Road now, down towards the Market Cross. Busily though the windscreen wipers were working, the town below them appeared wrapped in rain.

'Have you still kept up your music?' Mr. Higgins asked, after a silence.

'Yeah!' James said, 'I have as a matter of fact. I guess it's too strong and entrenched a love of mine for me ever not to keep it up.'

'I used to love to hear you play, you know. And Dorothy, who's not exactly the most musical person in the world, also loved to hear you. Why, when we used to see you as a lad, playing your mouth-organ on the porch of "The Cedars", we made up a name for you.'

'What was that?' asked James, nervously.

'Harmonica's Bridegroom. You seemed so in love with the instrument, and so dedicated to it, too.'

'Harmonica's Bridegroom!' James repeated. They were rounding the Cross now. All the figures of *ersatz* English folklore carved upon it were shaking their wet heads at him. 'Well, I can't object to that description of myself. But I'm separated from my bride now; I gave the instrument to a boy I knew here. I'd really like a reunion.'

'And I expect you'll soon have one,' said Mr. Higgins, though he couldn't, of course, possibly know whether he would or not. 'Now, James, when you arrive back at St. Jude's, take it easy, *please*! Do something undemanding and soothing. Be kind to yourself for the next few days. You see there are maybe other things in Tanbury now, that could upset you,' and he gave James a quick, apprehensive, meaningful look. But he didn't divulge its meaning, and James, for his part, felt too exhausted to pursue it. Though from

Mr. Higgins's tone the ominous, the to-be-feared emanated. 'And another thing – *don't* cut yourself off from your brother. You were such good pals in your boyhood.'

'I'll see,' said James. He looked away from the dreary streets they were travelling now and down at his own hands, capable-seeming and pink with exposure to wind and rain, a lover's hands, a musician's hands, perhaps a killer's hands. Could it be that Harmonica's Bridegroom was a double fiancé, his other bride being Death?

8

It was with a feeling of relief amounting to positive gratitude that – at the end of his lonely, troubled and interminable-seeming day – Dan heard the porter at Richard's *hostal* say that, yes, El Señor Cardew (he pronounced the name as if it were latinised Russian) *had* arrived. The *hostal* was the capacious, panelled, marble-floored second storey of an old town house in the Calle de Hortaleza. Behind it began that labyrinth called Chueca, indicated to him by Kevin last night as containing one gay joint after another. The porter sat underneath a too-brightly-tinted photograph of the King (who must be having an even more fear-ridden Sunday than Dan himself); he was engrossed in *El Pais* like that student of this morning; he said, reluctantly raising his head from the paper, that of course, if he wanted to, Dan could call on his friend in Room No. 7.

When, in reply to Richard's '*Si?*' Dan opened the door, he was delighted, almost to the point of tears, at what he saw. No one made rooms so untidy so quickly as his oldest friend. Richard – still at thirty-eight as much like some bedraggled but cheerful wading bird as he had been at the age of eight – was half-kneeling before a large suitcase which, in his own individual fashion, he was unpacking. Floor and bed were already generously littered with clothes and ill-assorted objects. Dan could see single socks, a typewriter out of its case (why?), a bottle of Spanish brandy, a toothbrush in curious isolation, films for a camera etc., etc.

'Oh, it's *you!*' said Richard, 'I was wondering when you'd be coming. Hope you hadn't any trouble finding this *hostal*. I'll just finish getting myself sorted out, and then we can go and have some dinner.'

'Sorted out, eh?' said Dan in affectionate amusement, 'we'll be here until at least tomorrow if we wait until you're in *that* condition. Why have you brought three fans with you, Rick? It's scarcely the height of summer.'

'Those fans aren't for me; I bought them for Cressida,' said Richard; Cressida was his small daughter and Dan's goddaughter – 'The man in the shop in Ciudad Rodrigo offered me three types, and I couldn't choose between them, so I bought one of each. They're all equally hideous, don't you think? All those gaudy flower-decked people painted on them. Still, Cressida hasn't reached the aesthetic stage yet. But I found something very nice for Kate on my travels.' Kate was his wife. He rummaged in the suitcase and came up with one of his sweaters in which, you could see, he'd wrapped his present. 'A really pretty old Portuguese plate. The Portuguese have such a beautiful tradition of painting on pottery and tiles. Kate's going to be absolutely thrilled with *this*.' He unfolded the jersey and dismay suffused his face. 'Oh, lordie, lordie, it's broken!' he said, 'and I'd thought protecting the plate with my jersey *such* a good idea. Look, Dan, it's now in about six pieces.'

'Gosh, that's a shame!' said Dan, thinking of all the inkbottles Richard had spilled at school, the pairs of spectacles out of which lenses had dropped, the watches that had ceased to work so strangely soon after they'd been given him, 'maybe you could find another in Madrid? There's this wonderful market here, the Rastro; I visited it this morning. Full of old plates and stuff.'

'The Rastro's only held on Sunday mornings, and I don't know whether I'll be here next Sunday,' said Richard, 'and also I paid a lot of money for this *particular* plate, so nice was it. But,' and his nice face brightened, 'you know how clever Kate is with her hands; she could maybe put it back together with glue or something.'

Dan thought this would be a well-nigh impossible task, but aloud said that Kate well might be able to do so, and Richard must be careful to keep the fragments together. He felt somehow heartened by the episode, selfish though this was of him; after the miserable thoughts of the day he was restored by it to what is called – and he himself called – normality.

'Oh, I'll leave the unpacking till later on,' said Richard, sitting down on one of the few available spaces on the bed, and wiping his brow. 'But, Dan, what a trip I've had! It's been wonderful – Galicia, Portugal, then back into Spain via Ciudad Rodrigo – and on to Salamanca and dear old Professor Olmedo Martin.' Richard was a lecturer in Comparative Philology (Romance Languages) at London University. 'Once again, though, I think of all the things I don't know, and will go on talking about as if I do. The Galician language, for example – there's a field of study for you! . . . Anyway . . . what sort of time have *you* been having here? Madrid can't have been so very pleasant today with all the Fascists converging upon it.'

'No, they made a pretty unpleasant sight!'

'And Madrid's such a lovable city,' said Richard, 'and with so splendid an anti-Fascist past. Is it the demonstrations that have made you look so sad, Dan? Or something else? I noticed a sadness about you the moment you entered this room.'

'Did you?' Dan was glad to have this chance so early on in their meeting of telling his friend his story. 'Yes, something is bothering me apart from the demonstrations. Rick, I must tell you about it. You see, last night, out on the Paseo de Recoletos, I met the most remarkable boy . . .'

'Oh, Dan!' Richard was looking at him just as he'd imagined he would do – quizzically, ruefully, 'why don't you give up meeting all these "remarkable" boys?'

'Let me tell you what happened first, for God's sake, before you start giving me advice,' said Dan, 'I was drawn to this boy because walking up the Paseo I heard the sound of a harmonica . . .'

'Well, that certainly *is* a strange story,' Richard said when Dan had finished; for all his garrulousness he was a good listener, 'I wonder *when* your boy met James, and *why* James gave him the mouth-organ. And also why, *why* . . . Kevin, you say he was called, couldn't bring himself to tell you personally about it all. Because he clearly couldn't. That must be why he sneaked off in the middle of the night, leaving behind him the harmonica as a sort of explanation.'

'Yeah, those questions have tormented me all day long,' Dan sighed (but how good it was to be talking them over with a warm-hearted friend of almost lifelong standing). 'But one deduction can be made, can't it? That Kevin fits in somewhere to the tragedy of what happened to James this time last year.'

'It would seem so,' said Richard slowly, 'though I hope you have ruled out the possibility of James and this pick-up of yours having been lovers? James is as "straight" as they come!' He looked at his travelling-clock standing at an unstable angle on the floor. 'It's getting on for Spanish dinnertime,' he said, 'let's go on discussing the matter over a good meal. I bet you've been so busy brooding that you haven't been able to eat a proper meal all day.'

'I'm afraid you're right,' said Dan.

'Well, eat one now, won't you, Dan? If only to keep me company. I don't want to feel like a greedy schoolboy! I know a very nice *mesón* near the Plaza Mayor, and we can walk to it, which will be good for us.'

This was the Puerta del Sol, Richard announced, the very heart of Spain. Here, earlier in the year, many thousands had stood in silence in their protest against February's attempted coup, against neo-Francoism, and in heartfelt affirmation of the so recent demo-cratic constitution. Behind the Puerta del Sol lay the grandest part of Old Madrid. The two friends walked up a street that resembled a canyon – with balconies like birds' nests in the rock-face – and so into the Plaza Mayor itself. 'Grand' was certainly an apt word for this raised, colonnaded, symmetrical square, lavishly floodlit so that it seemed to be the set for some *opera seria*, and even at this latish hour full of strollers. Across it, from its south-west corner, floated an inspiriting, almost mystical sound – of Andean syrinxes, accompanied by small, urgent drums and strummed guitars; the marriage of strains such as the very builders of the square must often have heard to those that their younger brothers and sons would have come upon in the mountains of South America . . . What had it been about the New World, Dan wondered, that had transformed popular music so; in both North American folktunes (the great love of James) and in South American ones passion dictated every note, and every note in turn dictated passion. However, though he looked longingly in their direction, Dan did not go up to and listen to these wide-and dusky-faced players with their straight, jet-black hair and big-brimmed hats. Maybe *one* encounter with a street musician was enough for a short visit to a city?

Richard led Dan down a flight of steps into another canyon – of leaning, ochre-coloured cliffs at the foot of which were many caves, the famous *mesones*, ramified cellars full of great vats and bare tables and lively people. In some there were music and singing to entertain you while you ate or drank. In another an elaborately decorated hurdy-gurdy was being turned by a man with a large grin on his face. Richard's *mesón* stood a little detached from the more obviously tourist-orientated ones. Soon the two of them were sitting in a dark, intimate corner, like contented cell-mates. Richard ordered for them both creamed spinach, to be followed by chicken cooked in garlic, and salad, and a large carafe of Rioja, a wine the colour of melted rubies.

'So what do you think of Spain so far?' Richard was asking him, rather as if he personally could make adjustments to the country to suit any requirements Dan might have. Perhaps knowing about its language gave you a proprietary feeling over a nation, Dan reflected, just as knowing about the traumata behind his speech defect tempted you to have over a patient. Funny, he continued inwardly, how we three friends, the 'Unholy Trinity', as sarcastic Mr. Dawes at the Grammar School so predictably called us – Jason Fletcher, Richard Cardew and myself – have all in some way devoted ourselves to language – me to difficulties in using it, Richard to its different forms, Jason to its deployment in the interests of the most vivid communication of current topics. 'Oh, I like what I've seen of Madrid pretty well,' he said, thinking of the judicious sight-seeing of the morning, 'but leaving aside the episode we've been analysing . . .'

'Which I bet we won't for long,' Richard interjected.

'There have been the demonstrations. Rick,' he repeated Kevin's question, 'what does it feel like to *be* those making them?'

Richard's mild, short-sighted eyes lit up at Dan's words; he'd always enjoyed discussions of such subjects, as perhaps only educated middle-class Englishmen, so *au-dessus de la mêlée* where violence is concerned, can. 'Well, I can't tell you,' he said, 'I can only make suppositions.' Then he gave Dan an anxious glance. 'Of

course I do appreciate how disturbing it must be for *you*, the associations it must have brought back,' he said, adding hastily: 'It isn't
wrong of me to speak like that, is it, Danny? We *can* be open about
the matter, can't we?'

'Of course!' said Dan, though inwardly he wondered quite how
open he liked others – yes, even Richard – to be. 'But maybe it
might be better to keep the conversation on the topic of Spain. I
want to be in a calm state of mind for tomorrow's paper.'

'Which I am much looking forward to hearing,' Richard said,
'well, to return to the Franquistas and their friends – now bowling
back in charabancs to Burgos or to Santiago de Compostella – on
one level, it surely isn't so very difficult to enter their state of mind.
For forty-odd years Spanish identity was bound up with profoundly
anti-democratic ideology and practice. Which could be said to have
worked.'

'Worked?' repeated Dan, shocked.

'In a pragmatic sense, undoubtedly. Franco kept Spain out of
the Second World War, though we may regret,' he gave a donnish
smile, 'the soldiers he sent out to Hitler's Eastern Front. He healed
the more obvious wounds made by the Civil War by building
up the country, later encouraging the tourism that made it prosperous. And if you say – as I'm sure you will – that he *created* the
Civil War, you'll find on reflection that that statement isn't really
very satisfactory. And then Spain kept itself free from most of the
worst confusions of the Cold War years. That was something to
be thankful for. So it preserved itself, to a very real degree, intact
from the difficulties of elsewhere. Its individuality is something we
still all love about it. And now, *now* Spain's having to become like
every other Western nation, and having to put up with a hundred
dissenting voices from within. Like every other democracy. So,
there you have it. Some Spaniards want the older, the thoroughly
Spanish Spain back.'

Echoes, terrible echoes in Dan's head! He shut them out – or
tried to – by saying: 'But they must remember the tyrannies of the
Franco regime.'

'"Remember"'s a difficult word,' said Richard, 'some are not
remembering at the moment, they're swept up by other emotions
than memory of particulars; others *do* remember the tyrannies

you speak of, but find that, when put into context, they aren't as bad as – say, disorder.' The waiter set down before them two bowls of creamed spinach; little slices of toast stood in these, like rocks in a lake. 'Don't look at me with such shocked eyes, Dan,' he said, 'I'm not expressing *my* views – or, God bless them, those of my Spanish friends.'

'But you're finding excuses.'

'Not excuses, explanations! You're determined to see the demonstrations as a manifestation of Evil. And no doubt there is evil abroad among the Fascist groups here though I dislike such phraseology – but I don't believe it's ubiquitous.'

'But I saw the arrogant smirks on the demonstrators' faces,' objected Dan, 'I heard the timbre of their shouts. You're being too academic and deliberately "understanding" about the whole thing, Rick. Too much the comparative philologist,' he added, though without malice.

'And *I* say that *you* looked and listened with eyes and ears over-conditioned by your private past. You were thinking – well, of James and Jason etc., etc. Undeniable? But let's talk about other topics. How's your spinach?'

'Delicious,' answered Dan, for so it was.

'And let me fill up your glass. You certainly gulped down your first. Rioja's the most comforting wine in the world.'

'Well, I certainly need to be comforted. It's James's birthday today – on top of everything else; oh, my memory has really been hyper-active today! Richard,' he knew that his tone was nervous, pleading, 'later – when we've finished eating and drinking – I'd like to try to find Kevin.'

'To try and find *Kevin*!' said Richard, laying down his spoon in astonishment, 'but how can you? It'll be very late . . .'

'I doubt whether that's a problem as far as he's concerned.'

'And also, not only do you not know where he lives, you don't even know his surname.'

'True, but I think there's a way. You see, I've a list of gay clubs' – he hoped he didn't say this too coyly or apologetically, 'and if we went round them, I don't think it'd be so very hard to track him down.'

'We?' said Richard, 'so you're wanting me to accompany you?'

'I'd be pleased if you did, Rick. I don't think you'll be so very shocked by what you'll see . . .'

'Oh, I don't know about that,' said Richard, 'I'm bourgeois and respectable down to my toe-nails. Our nocturnal tour'll be like Dante following Virgil, won't it?'

'Only remotely, I would say,' said Dan. Certainly he felt too confused to be conscious of any Virgilian properties in himself.

'Well, after my last mouthful of food and drink, I'll give you an answer, but *only* after!' Richard, however, contemplated the matter for a pause of at least a minute and a half. 'I suppose you'll have no peace of mind until you find this boy?'

'No,' agreed Dan, 'though maybe I also won't *after* I've done so! But light may just be shed on those events of a year ago. And I still need that light.'

'I can understand that,' Richard said, 'I must admit I find it hard to understand how Jason came to write that article he did – or how he even knew certain things in it. Sometimes I've thought that that fight between James and Jason in the school cricket pavilion began more things than it settled.'

'I know; I've thought that too,' said Dan, glad to hear his own idea from someone else's lips. But why, he thought, *should* the struggle have persisted? For what an unequal combat, to any objective eye, it appeared: Jason abundantly talented, and well-educated, successful, prosperous. And James . . . always destined to be none of these things.

'While on the subject of Jason . . .' Richard began. Then he stopped.

'Yes? On the subject of Jason, what?'

'Oh, it can wait,' said Richard, clearly not wanting to continue, 'we've gone over enough old ground today, Dan. We're away from England, in *Spain*. Haven't you been taken out of yourself at all by anything you've seen here so far?'

'Oh, yes,' said Dan, 'there was the monastery church of San Antonio de la Florida which I visited this morning.' He gave an apologetic laugh. 'But even there I was reminded of James.' . . .

He had walked to where the city of Madrid unwarningly falls away to reveal an untidy tract of grassland and trees. He'd descended a flight of steep steps carved in the clay escarpment and found himself crossing the railway lines that make for Atocha station; somehow their messy fringes, their prospect of scruffy but pleasing tall old houses and bleak, slab-like, modern apartment blocks had made him remember what he'd realised in the Paseo last night: that he, a Northern European, was in *Southern* Europe. And then – there it had been, the little church that was his destination – rather too near a traffic roundabout, and something of the colour and shape of a vanilla pudding, but of delicate proportions and compact shape which suggested that tranquillity could be found within.

The story that Goya had illustrated in the frescoes on the inside of the church's cupola was, to Dan's rationalist mind, preposterous enough. St. Anthony had journeyed from Padua to Portugal, where his old father had been wrongfully accused of murder, to resurrect the victim so that he could speak to an assembled crowd about what had actually happened.

By a master-stroke Goya had chosen to depict all his diverse company – saint, victim, sinners, worshippers, fair-people, peasants, aristocrats – standing before meticulously painted railings running the entire length of the bottom rim of the cupola. So that they all appeared, no matter what their attitude or cast of eye, to be gazing down at any visitor to the small, cool, solemn church (and now at Goya himself in his tomb). Dan studied first of all the representation of St. Anthony himself; he was holding out a thin but powerful hand towards an astonished group among whom was the ghastly form of the murdered man himself, bemused, piteous. On either side of the saint and those with whom he was directly concerned, a variety of women, boys and older men presented themselves at the railings against a background of wild, jagged rocks. Their wide faces and vivid, grotto-like eyes defied visitors to surrender to acceptance of time. They were the Spanish people Dan had seen yesterday and even that morning, in cafés, bars, on the Metro.

Then he turned round, and – his heart was suddenly painful in its beating. Opposite St. Anthony, dominating all those on his left and all those on his right, including beautiful young women and uncertain but stubborn young men, James arose; wearing a tunic, his stance sturdy with feet set wide apart on the ground, his hands asymmetrically and confidently outstretched, his head thrown back so that deep-set eyes could take in both distant saint and the sky above the rocky mountains, and transport consuming his strong, osseous face. He was the figure now known as *El Ecstático*, and he was James in moments of triumph, fulfilment – after playing one of his instruments well; after accomplishing a chosen task in house or garden; after a happy experience in the countryside. And surely Dan's Kevin-of-the-night must have seen this look on James's face, and loved him for it.

And now *El Ecstático*, his *Ecstático*, was hidden away in a barren, hygienic fortress, prevented – through the kindest of surveillance – from having opportunities for exultations.

' . . . You did like James, didn't you?' Dan asked Richard, for he had never been sure.

Richard took his time about replying. In fact he had been thinking about the piece of gossip concerning Jason Fletcher which his father had relayed him, and which, touching Dan (and James too) so nearly, once more, was certain to upset them both. Maybe he would not mention it even tomorrow; would leave it until his and Dan's return to England.

Richard was telling him that yes, of course, he liked James, but the answer was not so important to Dan as he'd thought. Because he was beginning upon a journey through the more recent past to recover his brother – going back first to a spring weekend of six years ago (in the year, in point of fact, though neither Dan nor James had paid much heed to the event, of Franco's death).

PART TWO

I

On stepping out into the yard in front of Tanbury station that Friday evening, Dan was agreeably surprised to see his brother waiting for him with the car. There he was, sitting in the light and warmth of the battered little VW, reading a newspaper he'd propped against the steering-wheel. Kind, thought Dan. True, it was raining – or more accurately, cold squalls of rain were being blown from the countryside into the town; true, it was his first visit to Tanbury for over six weeks. But such factors would not necessarily mean that James would meet his train. Absence crowded with meetings with strangers always makes you see your relations and friends with sharpened eyes. And now, James looks – said Dan to himself, hurrying to where the car stood – like a careworn boy. His tousled hair and actual physical attitude make him seem younger than his twenty-nine years, but the lines on his face, and more especially beneath the eyes, suggest the worries of a man quite a deal older.

'Well, this *is* a good welcome,' Dan said, 'I certainly wasn't relishing a wet walk to "The Cedars".'

'Oh, well,' said James carelessly, though obviously pleased at Dan's reaction, 'I'd got through all my jobs for the evening, so I thought I might as well tool down here. Besides – long time no see!'

'I was hoping to have come last weekend,' said Dan – though 'hoping' was surely mendaciously strong – 'but I did come back from the States to find a tremendous backlog of work. And then, of course, I had to write up the American visit itself.' 'Of course' was not the aptest phrase either; James had never had to write up a report in his life, and was surely very unlikely to.

'So now,' Dan added, perhaps a little too jauntily, as James started up the car, 'I can really relax.' Indeed so somnolent was the atmosphere of Tanbury, and of 'The Cedars' in particular, that there was little else that he *could* do.

'It's all right for some, isn't it?' observed James, 'I never come to the end of *my* work. Only to pause, like tonight. Right now, for example, I'm making new doors for both the woodshed and the coalshed, and bloody difficult it's proving. The previous doors were completely rotten – the wood came away in your hand; it was like a fucking insect sanctuary.' He made it sound as if the rottenness of the wood was, somehow, if at a remove, Dan's fault. 'And then at the beginning of this week Pappa developed a bad throat, and made a tremendous to-do about it, as you might expect. Dr. Cardew wasn't all that much help, so the burden fell on yours truly. He's better now, but has fallen behind with his work, and that hasn't made life any the easier for *me*, I can tell you.'

It's so long since James has had a normal job – one which demands that he turns up at a certain time and does work that fits in with other people and meets their requirements – that he's forgotten what one is like. Imagine *him*, said Dan to himself, having to deal with the psychotic demands of poor, spluttering Peter Woodward, or having Dr. Banyard breathing down his neck, or those endless GLC questionnaires to fill in. But Dan let him grumble self-approbatingly along while he drove the two of them round the Market Square, dominated by the sombre 19th-century clock-tower, and so into the Horse Fair. Eventually he said: 'Well, I'm sure you could put at least a few of those tasks to one side this weekend, James. As you said, it's a long time since we saw each other. Isn't there something diverting we could do?'

'I don't know whether *you'd* call it diverting,' said James, his words all coming out in a rush, 'but it happens that I'm playing with some friends in "The Pig and Whistle" tonight. There's a notice about me and the others in the local rag – take a look, it's open at the appropriate page.' He pointed to the newspaper he'd thrown on the floor.

Dan did – though looking at printed matter in cars always made him feel slightly sick:

'At the "Pig and Whistle" tonight', he read,

> 'starting at 9 o'clock (if you're lucky!)
> "Folk" for ALL Folk
> James Varney and the Mighty Handful'

'Well,' said Dan, 'fame at last!' He regretted the remark; not only was it facetious, it was patronising. Then: 'Does Pappa know you've taken his nickname for his *oeuvre* as the title of your group?'

James grinned: 'No; did you think I'd tell him? But it's no problem keeping things hidden from Pappa, is it? He scarcely notices other people's movements unless they directly concern him.' This was so true it did not need agreement. 'What I was wondering,' James was continuing, 'was – if you'd like to come along tonight, Dan, and listen to us.'

Dan was so used to being excluded from his brother's social life that for a minute he wondered if he were only being asked out of politeness. Then, glancing at his brother at the wheel, and seeing that – for some reason – he very much wanted him to come, he said: 'That's a terrific idea, James. Though won't Pappa . . . ?'

James grinned again, 'I've already warned him that you and I might go out tonight after our meal. You've blotted your copy-book already, Danny-boy, by visiting America, so your just going to hear American folk-music can hardly seem the crime it might have done a month or so back!'

'The Cedars' looked its usual aloof self, though since James had made looking after it his full-time job, its gates and drive and porch were in far better condition than at previous stages of its history under the Varney family. And – 'I've made something bloody good for dinner tonight,' James announced as he took Dan's bag with a swing of the arms and locked up the car, 'partly to give me energy for tonight's "do"; partly,' and he gave him a half-mocking nod of the head, 'in honour of the Prodigal Son's return. And it's none of Mamma's old veg. food either. It's a proper chicken casserole.'

Pappa was, self-consciously, self-dramatisingly, waiting for his sons in the drawing-room, standing with his back to a sweet-smelling but declining fire of wood and peat. Behind him hung the portrait of himself when young, painted – once again – by his friend Friedrich Mayerhofer. At its foot the artist had scrawled the profoundly embarrassing words: 'Siegfried Reborn?' (Certainly, Dan would say to himself, the question-mark, if not the title, was justified.) Pappa, who looked, now he was in his sixties, like some captive Old Testament prophet in shabby mufti, was clearly in a peevish mood, and in his bright blue eyes there was a decidedly 'put-out' look.

'I was just wondering *where* you could possibly have got to, James,' he said, as they entered the room, 'I have not, in point of fact, actually measured the time of your absence by any clock, but it seems to me to have been quite *unconscionably* long.' He spoke as if the only possible cause for length of time away could be some mismanagement on James's part.

'My train was very late, Pappa,' said Dan, 'it stopped for almost half-an-hour at Reading – I don't know why.'

'Trains have a habit of being late; it's the way of them,' said Pappa, who was fond of tautologous statements of this kind, 'but one would have thought that, realising this, perhaps a telephone call from James from some nearby box,' he chortled sarcastically at the word as if he were speaking of some outlandish modern invention with which it was bold to be *au fait*, 'might not have come amiss. Instead of which I have been worrying.'

And so of course he might have been. That was the trouble with dealings with Pappa. Just as he had confirmed your darkest vision of his all-consuming egotism, he revealed that, in some corner of his being, he did care about and concern himself with you.

'Oh, well, here I am, Pappa, safe and sound,' Dan said, once more aware of striking a falsely hearty note, 'and it's good to see you again.' And he made himself kiss his father. For it *wasn't* good to see him again, not at all – and he had only to be a few minutes in this room, with its gloomy, ornate furniture, its ghastly pictures and its shelves of unappetising books, to feel a breaker of depression crash over him.

'This fire needs a lot of tending to,' said James, 'I spent fucking ages making it and then building it up. You've almost let it go out, Pappa.' Their father took no notice of this criticism – fires, though he had celebrated them in prose (in *The Sacrament of Grass* and again in the pamphlet, *Recovering the Slumbering Will*, where they served as a metaphor for a nation's regeneration), were, his silence suggested, quite beneath his regard. James now proceeded to give logs and peat expert pokes and blowings.

'America does not seem to have made any outward difference to you, Dan,' said Pappa, 'but then it is America's declared triumph that it can penetrate to the inner as well as the outer man.'

'I spent most of my time in hospitals and university lecture rooms,' said Dan, 'so I think I was immune to the more dangerous of its influences. Since I've been back, I've had my films developed,' he went on in a deliberately 'normal' voice, 'so I can show the two of you my slides of Washington and the Appalachians later.'

'That will be interesting,' Pappa said, smiling at his favourite son, 'and I shall certainly look forward to the exhibition and accompanying lecture. But I must add that they are unlikely to make me change my mind about the country you'll be showing me, and even less about its all-too-hegemonic sway. I have been – well, a man of England, a man of Oxfordshire, first, of course – but from early years a devout European.'

'I'd particularly like to see your snaps of the *Appalachians*,' said James from the hearth; he gave the name – surely, anyway, one of the most magical in the world – a feeling stress. And yes, at the time, as he'd gazed on the enticing, azure wall of the Blue Ridge, Dan had thought: it should be James who's looking on these, rather than me. For who has loved the music that comes from the country beyond that alluring ridge more than he? James's harmonica and banjo had then sounded in his ears.

'The photographs of the Appalachians came out well,' said Dan, 'we can have a show of them tomorrow.'

'The mountains – are they as beautiful as they're meant to be?' James asked – almost nervously, Dan thought.

'They're *no* disappointment,' said Dan. And indeed they had not been.

'That's good to hear!' Reassured, James gave an erring log a hard poke.

'If I may be so unkind as to break into this traveller's tale for a moment,' said Pappa, 'can I ask, Dan, whether you are party to this strange idea of James's that you should go and listen to what passes in some ears for music at a hostelry in the town?'

'Very much so,' said Dan, his enthusiasm growing by the minute, 'it's a long time since I heard James play.'

'Would that I could say the same,' said Pappa, 'hours of each day I rest from my literary labours to have my ears assaulted by his din. But to each man his own wilderness. So – if you *are* going to James's "recital", he all but laughed at the term, 'I propose that we eat soon. I hate a meal that has to be consumed with speed. No doubt, James,' – he spoke to his second son on the hearth rather as a magician might to a cat in his employ – 'no doubt that fire is a triumph of the pyrotechnician's art. But I would say that dinner must be our priority now.'

'The casserole's ready when we are,' said James, 'nevertheless I will go and do various things in the kitchen. I'll give *you-all*,' he used the southernism with a wistful emphasis, 'a call in a few minutes.'

Under Mamma's dominion the kitchen had rarely suggested order, and her one bearable dish had been a large nut-loaf garnished with basil. Things under James were very different; the table was neatly, imaginatively laid, with candles in much-polished candlesticks, and his casserole was well cooked and served.

'Tell me, you boys,' challenged Pappa, 'why it is that the United States, the great power of the free world,' he smiled derisorily, 'has produced no figure to compare with Shakespeare or Goethe?' James, across the table, cast his eyes up to the ceiling in mock-despair.

'Goethe himself said: *Amerika, du hast es besser . . .*' said Dan, all too aware that they had had this conversation many, many times, long before his own first visit to the States.

'I must beg, then, for once in my life, to part company with the Sage of Weimar,' said Pappa, 'anyway he did not live to see the New World in its so-called "prime".' Once more the vatic laugh. 'Too much worship of Mammon must be the answer surely! You noticed it?'

Dan entertained a vision of his healthy-faced, athletic-bodied American colleagues bowing down before graven images. 'It is a materialistic society in many ways certainly,' he said, despising himself for the cliché, 'but then *Shakespeare* was by all accounts a shrewd businessman, and Goethe in Weimar was hardly leading the life of a pauper, was he?' Only Hampton Varney, he felt like adding, lives in perpetual, sequestered shabbiness.

Whether defeated by this argument or not, Pappa was pleased to change the subject. 'Well, at least you haven't come home with an American *wife*,' he said.

Dan felt that his laugh was unconvincing. His sexual tastes and where they would lead him were much on his mind at the moment; indeed he felt he would like to discuss them with somebody for assurance, though not with either of his present dinner-companions. (And even his best friend Richard, so nice-minded, so happily married, would not be an ideal confidant!). 'I'd have had to have acted very quickly,' he said facilely, facetiously, 'American conferences and visits to hospitals don't allow you much time for *breathing*, let alone for anything else.' But other men *did* have affairs with women on such occasions . . .

'I expect *James* would have found time,' said Pappa, 'I've had one or two aggrieved 'phone-calls of late, Dan, from some worried parents. Your brother has been misbehaving himself with their – Christine, was it? or Marlene or Irene, I cannot recall the name, and neither perhaps can your brother.' James winked across the table, and Dan winked back. But as a matter of fact, he thought, Pappa has a certain affectionate respect for James's amorous life. So – their relationship was more complicated than he often gave it credit for being; it was not merely some Nietzschean master/slave one. Pappa, Dan reflected, had probably himself been an ardent lover in his own young manhood; there had certainly been every evidence of a strong physical and emotional bond between him and Mamma.

'Music at "The Pig and Whistle",' said Pappa, as they all rose from the supper-table, 'that should mean tavern-music on a consort of lutes such as Sir Thomas Browne eulogised so memorably . . . not *American* vulgarities. Nonetheless, James, I wish you success tonight.'

The things we haven't talked about, thought Dan, stacking up the plates – my work, Pappa's work, James's lack of orthodox work; my lack of a female companion, Pappa's friendlessness, James's erratic, predatory substitutes for relationships. But, of course, of these subjects we never *will* speak!

The ceiling of 'The Pig and Whistle' was very low and was supported by Jacobean beams of blackened oak; the floor was flagged and uneven, and cushioned settles were arranged against the walls. In the centre of the area to the left of the bar burned a fire, even

better than James's at 'The Cedars', its flames leaping up towards
the copper hood which, glowing, gave off both light and heat for
the benefit of the patrons.

'James Varney and the Mighty Handful' had been allocated a
generous corner of the room in which to make their music, and,
when Dan and James arrived, the 'Handful' were already estab-
lishing themselves in it. In the dim lighting of the pub they all
looked to Dan curiously alike, with light-coloured longish hair and
untidy beards and dusty jeans, and with tankards of beer either in
or to hand. There was but one microphone ('The Pig and Whistle',
not being large, presented no acoustics problem) and James went
up to and slapped on the back the young man now adjusting it.
'Hey, there, Charley,' he said, 'I don't think you've met my brother,
Dan, have you? He's come here to *listen* to us, for his sins.'

Charley came forward from the mike, and gave Dan a sort of
cowboy salute. And his verbal greeting was even more unexpected.
'James here is pleased to tell me that you're *his* brother,' he said,
'but *I* say: you're *my* brother too. Like James is also my grandfather
and I'm probably your eldest son.' These Theban utterances were
delivered in a strange Brummy singsong into which some gener-
alised American had been injected, and Dan was quite at a loss for
a reply. However he was given little time to search for words. 'So
you've come to hear us play, have you? Now *Dan,*' he emphasised
the first name in brotherly fashion, 'you're under no obligation to
listen to us, and you just remember that, man, you just remember
it – whatever James here may say to the contrary. No obligation.
Quit the pub now, if you want to, or stay and drink yourself silly
instead. Or read a book, or play dominoes, or go out of your
mind for a while. But you're under no obligation to *listen* – get
it?'

Dan very much hoped he would survive the evening without
doing the last of these recommendations. Clearly the man didn't
know anything of the reality behind the term 'out of your mind';
James, for his part, was just a little embarrassed by his pal's late
sixties pseudo-Californianisms because he said: 'Oh, if Dan says
he's come to hear our music, then he's come to hear our music.
My brother's the most resolute person I know. Danny, Charley
here is the lead-guitarist, Pete *here* is second guitar. And that is

Tommy, percussion, and this is Ron, vocals – and also, when he's
tired or inspired – fiddle. Me I reckon you know already!'

Dan gave somewhat bashful smiles all round, and was, truth to
tell, much relieved when the Handful began to discuss the order
of the night's programme. It was as it had been at school – James
the maverick was far, far better than he at easy association with
promiscuous others, at plunging into that common lake of badinage, jokes, small-talk etc, which waters so much human communication. His own inability so to plunge had been perhaps the
main reason why Dan had so treasured the friendships of Richard
Cardew and Jason Fletcher. Maybe also a reason behind his newly
acknowledged sexual predilection.

Dan found himself a seat – an old rush-bottomed chair – near
the fire. He held in his right hand a pint-sized mug of cider and
tried to feel at ease. But what if he didn't like the performances?
Could he successfully conceal this from James? He rather doubted
it.

Presently two girls sat themselves down on stools beside him.
One was a voluptuous twenty, her dark hair swept abandonedly
up to meet a Spanish comb, her face a moist mask of exotic make-
up; her companion, by chosen contrast, was thin, spectacled and
fidgetty (though undoubtedly her stool would be uncomfortable)
and was perhaps her younger by a year.

'That's *him*,' whispered the voluptuous girl loudly, '*there* he is!'
She waggled in the direction of the band a finger that culminated
in a dayglo nail of livid orange.

'What, the one with the reddish beard?'

'Pooh, *James* with a *beard!*' snorted the first girl contemptuously,
'as if he'd need a beard to make himself look virile! No, James
Varney's that chap standing *behind* the others, wearing light blue
jeans and black polo-neck. He doesn't take part in *every* item,' she
explained with a grand air, that of an *illuminata* into the music
world, 'he has his *own* special numbers.'

The plain girl was now diligently, interestedly scrutinising James.
'You could tell, couldn't you?' she said cryptically.

'That he could break hearts like *that*, you mean?' said the first
girl, making a high, hideous noise, as of splintering wood, 'yes, I'm
very much afraid you could! Christine nearly pretended, you know.'

'Pretended?' repeated the spectacled girl blankly, and Dan shared both her bemusement and her curiosity, 'pretended what?' 'Honestly, Sandra, you can be so slow at times. Just think for a few minutes what a girl might pretend to keep a bloke? Anyway, Christine decided against it. For one thing she's basically too honourable; for another there was something about James Varney, she said, that you couldn't ever be sure of, something odd that . . .'

But – unfortunately – at that moment Charley's voice loudly buzzed into the microphone, drowning all the multifarious sounds of 'The Pig and Whistle' and its customers.

'Here we are again, people,' the voice said breezily, '"Folk" for the folk. That man skulking back there,' Charley jerked a thumb behind him, 'looking as if he's too good for us all is James Varney. And we here – modest, clean-living men and true – are the Mighty Handful.' And he proceeded to introduce his mates of the group and to announce the first three items that they would play.

These were an old Okie song from the Depression, 'If you Ain't Got the Do-Re-Mi', that Bob Dylan/Johnny Cash song from *Nashville Skyline*, 'If You're Travellin' to the North-Country Fair', and the white spiritual popularised by Ronnie Lane, 'It's Jesus on the mainline,/Tell Him what you want!' The Handful played well and animatedly, but Dan couldn't help feeling that really they imitated a little too conscientiously the singers on the records they'd been studying.

But maybe this was carping. For the music certainly brought back to Dan the long straggle of gaudily lit, one-storey commercial buildings that are strung along the road on the outskirts of every American town, brought back too the wild countryside that crashes on to these roads' shoulders when these have come to an end. And brought back virile but pliable-looking young American men glimpsed in bars or in passing cars, innocence and experience united in their easily-manifested sexuality.

Then Dan found his attention wandering away from the band and their songs, back to the conversation of the two now rapt-seeming girls. The voluptuous one, the curious Sandra and the absent Christine, who had so nearly 'pretended' – they had strongly responded to James – and why? Because of *his* response to *them*, surely; to them and to *all* their sisters. Whereas for Dan girls had never existed as an infinite, fascinating, diverse multitude. Now and again one had occurred – that was the appropriate verb – whom he'd felt a certain inclination, a certain obligation to take out. Oh, those terrible, terrible takings-out! Now he had at last ventured down the Other Road there would be no need for any more of them. The chilly strained hours in restaurants, deliberating over wines and dishes in order to earn smiles and complimentary remarks which he didn't, at bottom, want! And hours, too, in theatres and cinemas, clubs and parks. There had, of course, been Sorrel Williams. Sorrel had been, no, *was* different. (Someone had said she might be in Tanbury this weekend.) But she had not been interested in *him*.

. . . Now Charley was speaking to the pub audience again: 'And now for the man himself, for James Varney. *He* says he's shy, *we* say – but ssshh! don't let him hear! – that he's simple – but he doesn't like to make the announcements himself. So who does the task fall to but muggins here? James Varney will play for you-all, "Black Mountain Rag", "Raggerty Annie", and an instrumental version – for the bloke *can't* sing, not to save his life, let alone ours – an *instrumental* version of another white spiritual "There Ain't No Grave Going to Hold My Body Down". Thank you!'

Whereas the other players had all been obviously mindful of their listeners, and, too, of their self-images, nurtured in long hours of concentration on favourite albums, James played as if he were the only person in the room, and were discovering music for himself – harmonica at his mouth, banjo strung to his body. His eyes ceased to be eyes but became rather pools where melody had enjoyed protoplasmic being. You felt he had in some way left himself, as sometimes one did when making love. Indeed his every attention to his instruments was a lover's to the loved one's body, intently charged, strongly tender. Dan found himself remembering what funny old Mr. Higgins the newsagent had said: 'My wife, Dorothy, and I call James "Harmonica's Bridegroom", you know, Dan. He conducts an affair of the heart with the harmonica, does your brother.'

For his first two items James served all that was driving and wild in the tunes; in the third – in which the harmonica had a particularly prominent part – he cried out with his heart, a heart like some bounding animal in a densely-treed, uninhibiting land.

And Dan remembered what had met his eyes after he'd ascended the first wall of the Blue Ridge which rises so sheerly out of Virginia – another ridge, with beyond that a glimpse of another, all a-shimmer with the haze of woods. Arousing in you Longing – but for what? And James's music was as the ridges, productive – in its rises and falls, its surgings and strummings – of Longing. Longing as an Absolute.

The rain was coming down no longer in squalls but in a steady fall. James's windscreen wipers worked busily as they drove away from 'The Pig and Whistle' back home. 'Well,' said James, as Dan had known he would do, 'what do you think of James Varney and the Mighty Handful?'

'The Mighty Handful were enjoyable enough to listen to,' said Dan, 'though I doubt whether they'll prove at all memorable. But *James Varney* was something very different. I'd forgotten how very *musically* you play.'

He turned his head to see how James had taken these words – for it was possible to offend him by compliments as well as by criticism. But no – pleasure was suffusing his face. 'I played well tonight,' he said, 'maybe it was because *you* were there, Danny.'

Dan was so unaccustomed to such remarks from his brother that all he could say was: 'It'd be nice for me to think that.'

There was a pause. The rain flew against the front of the car and beat upon its roof. Lights were on in the thirties semis that stretched their ugly, homely way uphill to where fields began and 'The Cedars' mournfully stood.

Then James said: 'So America really is an interesting country to be in, eh, Dan? I *must* see those slides of yours.'

'I certainly found it interesting,' said Dan, a little guardedly because he didn't want Tanbury-enmeshed James to feel jealous.

'Is it true,' said James slowly, 'that after all the years of Vietnam unrest the Americans are recovering their own musical heritage – Bluegrass, Dustbowl, Western Swing, Jugband?'

'I believe so,' said Dan. Though the hospitals and universities of Baltimore, Washington, and Richmond, Virginia, were hardly the best places for finding this out.

'Danny-boy, I want to go to the States so badly. I must try my luck

– after all this time – as a Bluegrass musician. That's one reason, I'm afraid, why I asked you to come to "The Pig and Whistle" tonight. I wanted you to know – with your own ears, so to speak – that I was good.'

'Well, I truly can say that I do know that now.' The beams of James's cornflower-blue eyes, swivelled upon him, seemed brighter than any car headlight.

'Playing in Oxfordshire pubs just isn't enough, Danny. Okay, it's fun, it gives people – including myself – a certain satisfaction, but I want to be giving out to those who really *care* about such music. Who don't just treat it as a way of whiling away an hour over a few pints.'

'Well, that's understandable enough.'

'It isn't as though Pappa would really miss my services if I were to bum off to America,' said James, slowly, ruefully, 'except in the most literal way. For him I'm a failure-turned-garden-boy.' It wasn't an altogether inapt description.

Dan said: 'Pappa's too engrossed with *Prospero* to notice properly all the many things you do for him and the house. Still, I believe that he *does* appreciate you.'

James was silent again. 'The Cedars' hove into sight. Is there more to come? thought Dan; somehow he felt there must be. Then James stopped the car in a pool-ridden lay-by some yards away from the entrance to their house, and – 'Dan,' he said, 'I'd like to be in Nashville, Tennessee, the month after next. I've been making inquiries among contacts in musical circles there, you see,' (and who were *they*, wondered Dan, but why doubt? – Bluegrass music was something James really did know about and he didn't) 'and then, a month ago I filled in the forms for a Visa. But to get the appropriate Visa will take some weeks yet, and you have to produce evidence of sizeable money in the bank to be given one. To show you're no hobo, I suppose . . . You'd lend me that money, wouldn't you?'

'Of course,' said Dan. He said it easily, readily. For surely there was no need for cogitation on the matter. He thought of James poking the drawing-room fire which Pappa had let go out, and being told that supper mustn't be delayed, and then thought of him – transported, ecstatic – as he'd played harmonica and banjo in a conventional old English pub. Yes, his brother must . . . must emigrate. For Music, for Longing.

'Dan, I'll never forget this as long as I live. Not that I'm surprised. I've always known I had the kindest, most sympathetic brother in the world. Maybe one day *I* can do *you* a good turn.'

'There's no need to think of it in those terms. Anyway, I'll be coming to visit you in Nashville; I'll be glad to have a little foothold in the States. I really took to the country.'

'Don't get me wrong,' James continued, 'I've liked looking after "The Cedars"; it's given me a quiet contentment, but . . . no excitement, no fulfilment. To be playing tunes of the open road and the lawless life, to be singing songs about virginal woods and loving girls, and then to spend up your energies on coal-house doors that no one gives a shit about – that's hard!'

'I can believe it,' said Dan, and indeed he could. James's life would have driven *him* quite crazy. 'Tell me – have you given Pappa any inkling of your plans?'

James shook his head.

'I suppose,' said Dan, anticipating another request, 'that I'd better prepare him for it. But that's going to be the most difficult part of the whole business.'

Dan undressed by the gas-fire in his room, and then, full of now heavy thoughts, climbed into bed. Even after only three quarters of an hour, the wisdom of his readiness to finance James's departure seemed far more questionable than it had back in the car with the rain pelting the roof. Of his brother's musicianship he had no doubt – though was he really in a position to make a judgement on this matter? – but concerning his temperament – quarrels with masters at school, with boys (that fight with Jason Fletcher in the cricket pavilion!), with work-mates, with bosses – James's career was studded with these like a night-sky with stars. How would he really fare in distant, unknown Nashville, Tennessee, with no Pappa and brother Dan to help him out? And doubtless there would be more entanglements – Dan heard again in his head that strange, splintering noise made by the voluptuous girl in 'The Pig and Whistle', indicative of James's treatment of women's hearts. Many a Tennessee girl would be, so to speak, making the noise before so very long, and, well, James *did* suffer as a result, if only at a remove.

Dan had retained the ardent reading habits of his youth, reading in particular a great deal of poetry (perhaps, he'd sometimes wondered, because this was a genre Pappa had never essayed). Tonight he had with him – ironically – a volume of poems by writers of the Fugitive School, from where but Nashville, Tennessee, and the book fell open at a lyric by John Crowe Ransom. It filled Dan with a strange and disquieting music, music very different from James's 'Black Mountain Rag' or 'Wildwood Flower'.

'We pluck the spindling ears and gather the corn.
One spot has special yield? "On this spot stood
Heroes and drenched it with their only blood."
And talk meets talk, as echoes from the horn
Of the hunter – echoes are the old man's arts,
Here come the hunters, keepers of a rite;
The horse, the hounds, the lank mares coursing by
Straddled with archetypes of chivalry;
And the fox, lovely ritualist, in flight
Offering his unearthly ghost to quarry;
And the fields, themselves to harry.
Resume, harvesters. The treasure is full bronze
Which you will garner for the Lady, and the moon;
But grey will quench it shortly – the field, men, stones,
Pluck fast, dreamers; prove as you amble
Not less than men, not wholly.'

Dan saw the harvesters at work in Oxfordshire – was ever a county more lovingly farmed, more suggestive of harmonious coexistence between man and nature than his own – with its honey-stone villages and gentle hills and rich meadows? Though in quite what harvesting were he or James engaged? But no spot on earth was without threat to itself; Dan's first months of life had been attended by German bombers flying over this amiable land, and Coventry had burned for many of his neighbours and acquaintances to see. And today, as every other day, it was lapped at by Disorder. To preserve, to conserve the good – that must be the hero's task, to dam against the destruction perpetually planned for unleashing. And, even in the knowledge of these plans, the time-honoured rituals of life, inherent and peculiar to the place, *must* be carried on, and by its inhabitants.

But then – counterparting the ritual – appeared the fox. To James the wild animal sang with a Southern accent and its paws were as plucked banjoes; to Dan well, maybe to Dan it had a boy's teasing eyes and Apollonian breast. But, because the fox sprang from the coverts of one's own countryside, it could not be ignored. But what rite presided at its death, what cruel reverberating echoes of horn would sound as it received its agonising mortal injuries? Yet Dan knew that for both James and himself the Elder Son's lot, that of the reaper, could not be – not yet. The greyness of evening had not yet begun to descend for them, though it was always later than you thought.

2

The fox of Ransom's poem asserted himself, not surprisingly, in Dan's dream of the night; it sat fiery-eyed on top of Mamma's coffin and howled defiantly, until *James* approached him, catapult in hand. Emitting a last horrible cry, the fox bounded off into the woods – surely Foxton Woods, for they climbed up a steep bank that rose above the parkland of an Elizabethan country house. With a lip-fart of irritation, James threw down his catapult and ran after the creature. And soon the trees and dense bushes had swallowed him up, just as they had, minutes before, the fox himself.

As he surfaced into waking, Dan heard – re-played in his head – that last number in 'The Pig and Whistle' concert, one in which James and the Mighty Handful had united. The tune had been a catchy one, and later Dan was to hear it pounding out from juke-boxes in Nashville cafés.

> 'There ain't no good in an evil-hearted woman,
> And I ain't cut out to be no Jesse James,
> And you don't go writin' hot cheques,
> Down in Mississippi,
> And there ain't no good chain gang.'

What romantic-sounding bars! How they made you long, despite their advice, for life beyond law. But lawlessness was lawlessness, Dan thought, as the forms of pillow and bedding became clearer to his eyes; it meant abandonment of universally agreed ways of communion with others, it meant – well, didn't it? – a refusal to heed the gentler and the loftier promptings of the psyche. Even the 'I' of this vigorous, rousing song had realised, caught up though he was in this ethos of thrusting and breast-beating, that he did not want this violent estrangement. After his dream, after his remembrance of the song, Dan could feel none of last night's certainty that it'd be a good thing for James to take himself off, out of the confines of his present life, to the unknown world of Bluegrass music. Why had he agreed so promptly to help him do so? He'd always found denial and refusal difficult. Nevertheless as he ate the breakfast his brother provided for them (Pappa was already up in his study, had already begun his morning's work on *Prospero*) – a breakfast of porridge, with thick cream and golden syrup, followed by toast and marmalade – he made a resolve that he would go before lunch to talk things over with Father Lalland. As on one memorable earlier occasion, he could think of no one else he'd trust more.

Dan always felt a great tenderness for his bicycles; from his boyhood onwards, they had, when he rode them well, given him the nearest waking approximations to those blissful moments in dreams when it seems possible to enter any element on its own terms. The bike he used this morning was not in fact the same one as that on which he'd ridden homewards from school alongside Jason Fletcher and Richard Cardew or raced James all the way downhill to Foxton village and manor-house, but it felt as if it were. For it was 'Bicycle' itself to which one was attached. Along the Horse Fair Dan now sped, thirty-two years old but riding like a boy, past the churchyard in which the almond-trees were in vivid pink blossom, into the market-square, full of canopied fruit- and vegetable- and junk-stalls, and so out towards the station and St. Jude's. It was a blustery spring morning of watery sun; the grass was brilliant after the night's rain and the soil in flowerbeds was still visibly moist and exhaled a delicious, loamy smell; fluffy, compact clouds were tossed across the sky, and all growing things – daffodils, tulips, boughs with burgeoning leaves – nodded, not with drowsiness, but with a palpable eagerness for an imminent fullness.

As he neared the Vicarage, Dan could not but remember that other ride he'd made to ask questions of Father Lalland, that May afternoon splendid with hawthorn, his seventeenth birthday . . .

Dan had neither seen nor heard that fight in the Pavilion, yet the words that had led up to it and the blows it had entailed had resounded in his ears all during his journey. James had had to be dragged off Jason, but not before he'd given him a cut lip, a black eye and a loosened tooth. And not before the reasons for the fight had travelled all round the school. What strange physical laws nasty gossip followed and proved!

Perhaps having to take part in a team game had put both James and Jason into bad tempers. Apparently James, who was, it had to be admitted, all too prone to making such remarks, had asked Jason whether he did not feel honoured to have been invited to Dan's birthday dinner at 'The Cedars' that night – 'to sit at the table of a real life author.' Jason had replied, facetiously enough, 'No, not particularly. It's *he* who should be honoured to entertain *me* – a real live author of the *future!*' Irritated, James had, to snub him, gone on to imply that the reason why Jason's father, a mere librarian, a paltry bureaucrat, took no interest in Hampton Varney's books, was because he was *unable* to appreciate them.

'He can appreciate them only too well,' Jason had replied, in a cold, measured voice, 'he knows that they're the work of a Nazi!'

Poor James! Unintellectual, innocent in so many ways, he had never made any connection between Pappa's writings and the isolation from both the cultural and the humdrum worlds in which his family lived, other that is than the one Mamma had so carefully and consistently presented to them since their early boyhoods – that like his great German Friend, Friedrich Mayerhofer, Pappa had been too much a man of vision to get on in this materially-minded society. Dan had for some years realised that this could not be the whole story – for one thing, anti-materialistic though he was, his father was a vain man who sought approbation, and yet what approbation ever came his way? Piecing together his father's statements of *weltanschauungen*, his memories, his writings (or what he'd been able to read of them), Dan had come to see that his father's sympathies before the War must have been, to say the least, equivocal. Further than that he had not ventured to direct his mind.

But Jason had. He had asked his own father, the mere librarian, about the career of Hampton Varney, and he had been able to come up with facts. So – foolish James! when he viciously but, as he thought, righteously battered Jason like a 'ram' made flesh, he was attacking someone who – from whatever motives – had spoken words in which truth was contained. (Even if they did not constitute truth itself.)

The cricket pavilion fight had ended Dan's own mental virginity. Now he *must* know. But who could he ask? His mother would only dissolve history, first into weeping, then into romantic tributes to the nobility of their father's temperament. There remained Pappa's only constant friend in Tanbury (and a good friend to himself and James), Edward Lalland.

Who, kindly, but directly, in his study, through the open window of which the scents of may and flowering currant and mock-orange-blossom had drifted, had told Dan Hampton Varney's story: his ideological affiliation with the Mosleyite movement (though he had never actually been a member of the British Union of Fascists); his admiration of and subsequent friendships with John Heygate and Henry Williamson; his correspondence with Knut Hamsun; his preoccupation with a Nordic alliance, with the fusion of German and English cultures; and his hot-headed, ill-informed rushing into print on these matters. An idealistic fool, it seemed, had hastened where a more ordinary man would have feared to tread.

And the fragrances from the garden had become for some minutes as the smell of sulphur. How would Dan ever be able to face Pappa again?

What Father Lalland went on to say was scant consolation, though offered as atoning matter. The revelation of the extent and nature of the Jewish persecution (something Pappa had denied – a homeland, a reservation of some kind was undoubtedly being found for such non-Nordic folk!) had upset him to such a degree that he was for many weeks familiar with thoughts of suicide.

Then Pappa had bravely defied tribunals and won acceptance for service in the Home Guard and in charitable work for English soldiers. So . . . but, no, Dan could not feel anything but anger and pain. The arrogance, the stupidity, the muddle-headedness, above all the *non-humanity* of it all! Who, seeing only a handful of photographs of ostracised Jews or Communists, could not at once place heart and attention *there*, on *them*!

'Don't blame him, Dan,' the priest had pleaded in his heavy, asthmatic voice, 'your father, you see, is a Man of Vision,' ('*Et tu, Brute*,' Dan had felt like exclaiming at this point) 'and he was therefore . . . therefore blinded to the realities behind the cause he espoused, the cause indeed, he suffered for. "Suffered", did I say? Dan, he suffers still. For all his solitary streak, do you think your father would have chosen *quite* such an isolated furrow to plough as that he does now? He has been disappointed in life, realise that; he deserves our compassion.'

But did he? A serious youth, Dan always instinctively responded to situations with moral questionings. Suppose, he'd now asked himself, that things had turned out differently, had turned out as Mosley and his supporters had hoped, and England had indeed shaken Germany by the hand. What then? Would Pappa have continued – and proudly – to churn out his romantic rhetorical apostrophes to sap and leaf, to Shakespeare and Goethe while the underfed, imported sweat-labour arrived from Eastern Europe, and English Jews were shoved on to cattle trucks?

'It's all very well for *you* to talk about compassion,' Dan surprised himself by saying, '*you're* a naturally – as well as a professionally – compassionate man. But what about – ' and he could not check the self-pity in his voice, '*me*? What about James? It's not so easy for us to be compassionate, I think. Also, don't *we* deserve pity as well? Think what it's . . . what it's like to have . . . to have discovered yourself to be the son of a man who . . . who went in for all *that*!'

It had been when delivering this last sentence that Dan had – for the first and, in any serious sense, the last time in his life – stammered. And this faltering delivery of it had shaped the course of his mature life.

When he'd recovered, Father Lalland had said: 'You and James have your own lives to make, Dan.' But this cliché, as Dan had thought at the time, is only partly true, *can* only partly be true; Edward Lalland had spoken it rather self-consciously, and he must have realised this too. For how can one *make* a life – claims from others must always be upon one, and what claims more powerful, more inescapable than those of the men and women who gave one life? Years later Dan was to read Robert Louis Stevenson's verse-motto to one of his fables:

> 'Old is the tree, and the fruit good,
> Very old and thick the wood.
> Woodman, is your courage stout?
> Beware! the root is wrapped about
> Your father's heart, your mother's bones,
> And like the mandrake comes with groans.'

The front garden of the Vicarage was riotous this morning – under trees, upon banks – with what Father Lalland always liked to call 'the sun's trumpeters': daffodils, jonquils, narcissi. In the long, curving driveway there were many puddles of rainwater, through which Dan, in a fit of boyishness, born of apprehension and memory, deliberately rode his bike. Cats and chickens were visible. The front door of the rambling, turreted, red-brick house was open to the outside world – Dan dismounted and rang its bell. No answer, but, from the kitchen regions at the back, voices could be heard, the priest's among them, raised in distinct distress. Oh, dear, thought Dan, I've come at a bad time, and yet if I don't raise the matter of James's departure now, I never will. And I'll let him go to the States, thus doing him great wrong. He stared into the cool, tiled hall with its vases of flowers and its samplers on the walls; the voices not only continued but rose, though he could not catch any words that explained the cause of the fuss, and he was just about to turn away, sadly, reluctantly, when the door at the far end of the distant passage opened and a fat chicken with fur all over its legs emerged, followed by an out-of-breath, red-faced Father Lalland and a rather younger man who, for all his comparative sophistication of dress and mien, featured him a little.

'Esmeralda,' the priest was now bending over and clapping

his hands behind the chicken's tail-feathers, 'will you *never* do as you're told? Will you *never* listen to orders? You've been exceedingly naughty, and you're not ever to go into the kitchen again. My sister Frances was not pleased.'

The chicken advanced a few irate paces into the hall and then came to a stop. The younger man then took over and shooed the hen with a certain violence until finally it fled the hall, fled down the steps and out into the garden. Shutting the door behind him with a look of malevolent satisfaction on his face, the stranger turned his head and took in Dan. 'Edward,' he said, 'in all this absurd confusion we've not so much as noticed that you have a visitor. One of the needy of the parish, I take it. An Oliver Twist who has reached his thirtieth year perhaps!' There was something faintly disagreeable about his suavely spoken mocking phrases.

'Dan,' said Father Lalland, 'what a pleasant surprise! An unannounced old friend is the greatest of treats. Unfortunately the morning has been consumed by Esmeralda's truculence, and so have my wits. She is the most individualistic of the chickens, I think.'

'The sooner her individualism finds expression in her sitting roasted and ready for carving on someone's lunch-table the better,' said the unknown visitor. He was a handsome man, Dan thought, with a face flushed as if by port, and crinkly, well-cut, dark hair amply punctuated by grey.

'Gerald!' remonstrated Father Lalland – and Gerald, Dan now remembered, was his younger brother, father of a beloved nephew – 'don't be so callous. And anyway the Baggy Trousered Chickens are *not* good for eating. Nor for eggs either, you know; their eggs are tiny and tasteless. But for intelligence,' and here he lowered his voice to a reverent, affectionate whisper, 'there isn't a chicken their equal.'

'So I've been told before,' said Gerald Lalland, and it was, Dan reflected impatiently, more than likely that he had been.

'The things they think of!' said Father Lalland musingly.

'I can't imagine *what* things,' drawled Gerald Lalland, 'well, Esmeralda, to dignify the bird with a name, presumably thought about coming into the house today, but if you consider that either a sign of intelligence or at all interesting in itself, you must have an even more peculiar view of life than I've given you credit for.'

'Dan can't be much interested in our domestic problems,' said Father Lalland, greatly to Dan's relief. 'Had you come to see me about anything in particular?' For he must have read the marks of anxiety upon his friend's son's face.

Dan said that he would be very grateful if Father Lalland could spare him a few minutes of his time. He had a serious question to ask him.

Sitting in Father Lalland's study, the window of which was again open on to a fragrant garden, Dan could not but feel extremely close to that anxious, seventeen-year-old self he'd been recalling; it was as if, indeed, with his plumpish face a little disfigured by pimples, his earnest brown eyes and his crew-cut, he was seated in the vacant wing-chair right beside himself now. The priest's study was not one which suggested learning; its books were not many, and were as likely to include, say, Gilbert White's *Natural History of Selborne* as theological discourses. Father Lalland – after all he *was* a brother of the Community of the Resurrection at Mirfield – presumably led an active spiritual life; he had once said over nut cutlets and elderberry wine at 'The Cedars' that every day he 'had to go for a quick swim in the Mysteries', but when he was not thus swimming, he seemed far more interested in the domestically pastoral than in the intellectual aspects of his calling. And he could display in the former, a gentle, practical concentration on issues that surprised those who had listened to his almost inaudible and inconsequential sermons or had heard him bumbling on about his baggy-trousered fowl . . . 'So, what is it you want to ask me?' he said to Dan, his tone as serious as Dan had said his question was to be.

Dan told him of James's confession and request of last night and his own response to it. When he'd finished Father Lalland was silent for a few moments; his large, veinous hands caressed one of those Victorian glass paperweights that contain a snowstorm. So that a tempest, representing to Dan the possible disorder consequent on James's decision, raged for him to see in that calm and comfortable room. Then: 'Well, tell me the *problem*, Dan,' Father Lalland said, 'because you have not done so yet. Do you realise that? James is a great lover of American folk-music, even *I* know that much, and, as far as I can tell, he's a talented musician. He's at an age when it's not only natural to be adventurous, it's to be expected; at that period of life I myself was in a Mission Field in Kenya. You, I take it, have perfectly adequate funds to meet James's wishes, otherwise you surely wouldn't have given him the promise you did. As for Hampton, I *think* he will be understanding, but if he were not to be, that should "cut no ice",' he pronounced the slangy phrase with an almost comic emphasis, 'should "cut no ice" with *either* of you, because we must not allow his selfishness to prevail. Maybe it has already done so over James a little too much. Therefore I ask you again, Dan: *What is the problem?*'

Dan did not look directly back up at Father Lalland; instead he turned his gaze and confronted again, it seemed, his perturbed, seated, seventeen-year-old self: 'It's hard to explain,' he said, 'it's just a *feeling* on my part. That it might not be good for James to go.'

'A feeling!' repeated Father Lalland, 'ah, feelings can have such a multiplicity of causes. May I suggest one for yours?'

'Please,' said Dan, almost nervously. Was this how patients felt towards *him*? Was he having a taste of his own medicine?

'That you want the person you've always been closest to in the family to stay where you can see him whenever you want.'

Dan started. He was astonished. This explanation had never occurred to him. Nor could he immediately accept it.

'But I've *always* wanted James to do what would make him happiest!' he protested, his voice probably betraying an inner distress at the priest's ideas. 'Of course I realise that up to now he hasn't had a very satisfactory life, but . . .'

'Not a very satisfactory life! A most *unsatisfactory* one – for *him*!' said Father Lalland, 'must he not – every time he was sacked from a job, for whatever reason – bad time-keeping, quarrels with a boss or a colleague – have felt a lance piercing his side? And meanwhile you, Dan, quietly ascended your professional ladder.'

'But not at James's *expense*,' said Dan, 'no one would have been better pleased than I had he made a go of a job.'

'Pleased? But for what reason?' demanded Father Lalland, almost tartly for so mild-mannered a man, 'would it really have pleased you so very much if James had become – something highly unlikely, I must add – a champion rep. for that toothpaste and powder firm he worked for?'

The seventeen-year-old Daniel Varney had disappeared now. His successor, alone in the room with these unanticipated questions, felt slightly giddy in the head. 'I didn't say, did I? that I wanted James to be successful in *that* job. Or in one like it.'

'Let's try to forget about being "successful", shall we?' said the priest. 'There is only one kind of success, and whether we attain it or not we will never know in *this* life. Believe me, Dan, I'm not trying to "get at you".' He delivered these last words just as he had done 'cut no ice'. 'I like you, I respect you, and I *know* you to be of honourable intention. I just want you to see things how *I* see them – which could indeed be a wrong way – but which may have more objectivity than has your own vision at present. You talk now of stopping James from going to America – where he longs to be, where he loves the music – and indeed you have the means of doing so. But you never tried to stop him from taking on jobs he could never enjoy or do well in. You never stopped him from his present half-life at "The Cedars".'

Dan bowed his head before this last statement. For it was correct, even if not entirely just. 'You're right,' he said, 'maybe I haven't been the best of brothers to James.' This, he realised, was his own uneasy self speaking; Father Lalland had not said this, and indeed went on to deny it.

'I would hate to imply that,' he said, 'rather, I think you love him *too* much. You love him, perhaps, without altogether liking him. That is a very difficult predicament.'

Dan clasped his hands tightly, painfully together, and bit back a longing to cry out. But he knew – as on that May day fifteen years ago – that the truth had been spoken in this room, and he was afraid.

'I must let him go to America, then?' he said.

'*You must keep your promise of last night!*' corrected Father Lalland, 'and when James has gone, then you must attend to your own situation.'

So does he know? Dan asked himself, his mind returning to the sexual Other Road. Probably! He must in the course of his pastoral

work have met many of my kind. Perhaps, in fact, he knew years
before I made my full admission to myself.

Dan thought swiftly of his current emotional preoccupation,
Jeremy, encountered at a party a short time ago, and gone home
with afterwards, of his merry, beautiful face, his darting grey eyes,
his sweetness of tongue as it french-kissed. And as he thought
thus, he knew that never, never could he present his homosexual
life as a problem – not to kindly Father Lalland nor to anyone else.
For in itself it was now *not* a problem, not as James and life at 'The
Cedars' were; it was merely the direction of his desire. (Though a
bringer of particular problems it undoubtedly would be.)

'So – keep your promise, dear boy,' bade the priest. 'And now I
think we'll go and partake of sherry in the drawing-room. We'll
warm you for your ride home, because despite the sunshine, the
breeze is cool.' He paused, clearly wondering if he'd said the
kindest things. '*Thank* you for confiding in me, Dan; I'm flattered,
and I only hope I've eased your burden a bit. And remember also
that James Varney has James Varney's life to lead – and by lending
him a bit of money you're enabling him more amply to do this.'

Frances and Gerald Lalland were in the drawing-room and they
joined Edward Lalland and Dan in the sherry-drinking. Gerald
who, it appeared, loved all things Spanish, was, so his siblings said,
a connoisseur of sherries, and this one, it transpired, was particularly fine. Nevertheless, Dan noticed, he downed his glasses rather
than savoured their contents. Dan thought – here's a businessman
who eats and drinks too much for his own good, and who knows
it. Frances Lalland, on the other hand, sipped her sherry as a bee
might nectar from a flower. She had recently been sent, all the
way from New England, she said, a very pretty piece of early
19th-century patchwork by one Nancy Macdowell of Pawtucket,
and indeed she seemed to have been translated by the gift into a
near-beatific state, which quite transcended the warmth given by
sherry.

No sooner had Frances Lalland finished her anecdote than
Gerald Lalland drawled: 'Though Tanbury is, I consider, a tedious
place,' he addressed Dan, cynical-man-to-cynical-man, 'I confess
to being glad to stay here for a while. For the tedium of life as
chief executive of one of our larger advertising companies and as

"breadwinner" of a claustrophobically small family surpasses even that of Tanbury.'

'Come, come, come, Gerald,' said Edward Lalland, 'what an impression you must be giving Dan. Your job, I concede, I would not care for, but you have a lovely wife and a lovely son. A boy,' his voice slowed and softened in loving memory, 'who took at a remarkably early age to the blessed Anglo-Catholic rituals. How he used to love to finger all my albs and cottas! "One day, Uncle Eddie," he said, "I shall be wearing these!"'

'Over my dead body he will,' said Gerald, 'anyway the lad's an uncomfortable-making mixture of milksop and mischievous sprite, and I'm not sorry to be away from him for a bit.'

'Gerald isn't as unfatherly as you'd think. He's brought us uncle and aunt a beautiful new framed photograph of our nephew,' said Frances Lalland, 'and there he sits, look Dan – on top of the grand piano.'

Dan diligently turned his head to look at him. And saw a picture of a youth in his late teens – of a quite exceptional sweetness of expression. Tender, dark eyes melted into his as he gazed upon them; one day, perhaps, he would be lucky enough to meet their owner. He was the sort of boy for whom . . .

'. . . But then,' Gerald Lalland was continuing, 'what *isn't* tedious in our age of *muflisme* as the great Flaubert called it. (Yes, Dan, time was when I read "Good Books".) If only I could be living in an era of adventure.' (Adventure! James's desire!) 'My own particular choice would be the Spain that began with *Los Reyes Católicos*. When the strong, obsessed men of wild Extremadura opened up a New World and found there a land even more wild than their own and a people as strong and as obsessed . . .'

Bicycling home, Dan let convincement conquer him. Indeed by the end of the day he had all but forgotten that he had entertained any reaction other than last night's readiness to assist James to a new, a fuller and therefore better life. He whistled as he biked along the Horse Fair, its fledgling chestnut-trees nodding even more vigorously in the wind now. The tune Dan whistled was 'Wildwood Flower' as rendered by James last night.

And then – at the corner of the street he saw her – Sorrel Williams, clad in a grey cloak and a grey skirt, and with her chestnut-brown hair free and shining. So the gossip was right, she *was* in Tanbury after all. Had he ever really been in love with her? he wondered. Certainly he had thought about her a good deal, including when in bed. And he had ridden over on his bike at nights to look at her lit-up bedroom window. When he'd learned that she was going out with Jason Fletcher, he had cried – real tears. But never had she excited him, had she filled with her image the entirety of successive days as Jeremy, for instance, had, was doing.

Dan did not slow down, rather he accelerated the bicycle until the point when, quickly swivelling his head round, he could see her as but a distant pencil-line of delicate grey.

James was doing something to the left-hand gate-post as Dan described an arc with his bike into the driveway of 'The Cedars'. 'Come a bit loose from its moorings,' James explained, 'the bugger! Dan, I've broken the news myself to Pappa about America. After all you've done, all you've promised to do, I didn't think it fair for *that* little load to be yours.'

'Well, thanks! And how did he take it?' But Hampton mustn't be allowed to be selfish, the priest had counselled.

'Oh, not too badly. I told him, also, that you were lending me the money. "That's just the sort of fool thing Dan *would* do," he said. "That's just the sort of generous, constructive thing he would do," I replied. Dan, don't ever think that I'm going to leave our friendship behind, will you? Because I'm not.' Rhythmically James resumed hammering at the recalcitrant post. 'Our friendship's been terribly precious to me, all these years, even though you may not have realised that. And it always will be. Those visits of ours to Foxton Woods! Sometimes I'd feel as if you and me and the harmonica I'd bring with me and the badgers we'd gone to watch were all one and the same. And that feeling I'll carry with me always wherever I go.'

'Me too!' said Dan . . .

Pappa said to Dan: 'So James has decided to go out to the Barbarian Empire across the Atlantic, and you, I gather, are enabling him to do so.'

'You could put it like that, yes.'

'An old Victorian music-hall song comes to mind,' Pappa said, 'you have doubtless read about the *cause célèbre* of the famous elephant, Jumbo, being separated from his mate Alice and shipped off to the USA?'

'No,' said Dan, 'I can't say I have.'

Pappa said: 'It's not as irrelevant as you appear to think. Let me sing you a verse from it:

'Jumbo said to Alice: "I love you!"
Alice said to Jumbo: "I don't believe you do!
For if you really loved me, and wanted to be true,
You wouldn't go to Yankee-Land and leave me in the Zoo."'

But Dan said: 'I think his decision to go to America is the best that James has ever made!'

3

For the next two years James wrote home – principally to Dan only – with a surprising regularity. His letters were chatty and warm and full of enthusiasm for the country in which his brother had generously made it possible for him to settle. Dan thought of these letters as proceeding from James's old boyhood self. And maybe Tennessee *was* the place where that self could best flourish. James described musicians he'd heard, animals he'd seen in the Great Smokies and – girls. Southern girls were surely the prettiest in the world; no wonder they'd inspired so many beautiful songs and tunes. As for his own career as a Bluegrass player, well, he was realising that he would have to be patient. Not a bad lesson for him to have learned. Response had been favourable though, talks of offers had taken place; so . . . 'Keep your fingers permanently crossed, Danny-boy!' Meanwhile it'd be as well if he were to take a job. By a happy chance the father of one of the girls he was going out with – in point of fact the nicest and prettiest of them all – was President of one of the biggest catering companies in the Southern States. He'd taken quite a shine to James, and thought there could be a good opening for him in his Sales section.

A few months after this particular letter James wrote to say that

he had – quietly, without fuss – married this President's daughter.
Her name was Cynthia, she was the best, the truest girl he'd ever
had the fortune to meet, and here were some photographs of her!
These showed a sun-kissed, snub-nosed face framed by long yellow
hair. Cynthia looked charming enough, Dan thought, if a little coy
and winsome. One of these days, James promised, he would see
her; Dan would be coming over to the States on one of his conferences, or James would have saved up enough dough to take himself
and Cynth for a holiday in England. (For this was in the days before
cheap flights!) And that Dan and Cynthia would get on like a house
on fire James had no doubt. But whether this was true or not Dan
was never to have the opportunity of finding out.

There was something else besides the snaps in this particular
envelope. What was it? Dan shook it, and discovered a cheque for a
sizable portion of the money he had loaned James. Dan was more
than surprised; he was *moved*. In the midst of his new-found happiness, James had remembered his brother with affection and gratitude. You couldn't ask for more.

After his wedding there was a protracted lull in James's correspondence. 'We have lost James,' Pappa boomed, not without a
note of morbid satisfaction, 'lost him to a universe of refrigerators
and drive-in movies and bank cards and fifteen-channel television.
The soil of Shakespeare he has, as it were, spat upon and spurned.
To say nothing of his own family.'

'Oh, nonsense,' said Dan, 'he's just immersed in other things at
the moment, and isn't that natural for someone just married and
building up a home? One of these days another letter will arrive
proving that James isn't lost to us in the least.'

Perhaps he'd spoken as he had because he also was immersed
in other things, and to an intenser degree than before or since.
He had embarked on an ambitious research project that came to
resemble a roundabout with the majority of the turnings-off *culs-
de-sac*; he had anticipated this – at least cerebrally – but nevertheless
still found himself gnawed at cruelly by doubts of his own intellectual judgement and capacities, and so despairing, day after day,
of ever achieving positive results. In the personal domain things
were, if anything, harder still. He had come – painfully – to realise
that just waiting for a lover to manifest himself at some party –

as Jeremy had done – was foolish, approached indeed a solipsistic view of life, which he, as introvert, was all too prone to taking. And so he began – at first with feelings of breaking some toughly resistant moral maidenhood – to pay visits to gay pubs and clubs, to embark, in other words, on that quest which still had not come to its end. As both his psycho-medical and his homosexual pursuits were matters it would be impossible to discuss with James, in either conversational or epistolary form, Dan became reconciled, month by silent month, to the probable fact that theirs was a relationship which belonged to the past. He was only glad that it had closed on a note of love and trust.

And then the letters began again. They were longer, looser, breezier than before, and often so stuffed with hyperboles in American idiom that it was hard to believe that an Englishman, let alone his own brother, had written them. He had moved to a new address – this was it! – in another part of Nashville, he was still prospering at his work for the catering firm, and, as well as playing guitar, harmonica and banjo with success at private functions, had – and with good grounds – higher hopes than ever of making it professionally. 'So – keep your fingers permanently crossed, Danny-boy!' he said again. After all wasn't Nashville 'Music City U.S.A.'?

There was, Dan allowed himself secretly to admit, something he did not at all care for about these letters, glad though he was to get them. Indeed his aversion to parts of them led him to conceal them in their entireties from Pappa, whose reactions to them would be all too predictable. Was it that the boasting was by no means as ingenuous as its youthful phraseology might suggest? That it contained a strong element of gloating. For here was James, the no-good bum, the dunce, the man sacked from a variety of jobs and always despised by his father – not merely making good, but leading a far more varied and exciting existence than the virtuous, ever-respected Dan. Moreover Dan had acquired from both his parents and his educational establishments a pronounced puritan antipathy to the culture that James now so lavishly eulogised – that of country clubs and swimming-pools, barbecues and hell-raising sports cars. Were these the only rewards for the present-day man of adventure, for the social buccaneer? Could he not achieve any rousing dominion of the *spirit*? Such reflections were the times

Dan came his closest to the *weltanschauung* of *The Sacrament of Grass*.

About eighteen months ago the first opportunity for many years to visit the States had come Dan's way. He was invited to read a paper – on the efficacy of a particular method of treating stammerers – at a conference in Charlottesville, Virginia. Charlottesville, on the other side of the Blue Ridge Mountains from James's Nashville! Excitement at the prospect of being able to see his brother after so long a period made Dan, within an hour of his acceptance of this invitation, find out his telephone number from International Directory Inquiries, and then ring him up.

James's manner over the 'phone was not at all what Dan had expected. He sounded neither surprised nor pleased to hear Dan's voice, though a long period had elapsed since their last, rather forced Christmas conversation. A conference, eh? – well, there was always one of some kind in Charlottesville, wasn't there? Charlottesville and Nashville weren't anything like as close as Englishmen imagined – the whole bloody Blue Ridge lay between the towns, didn't it? Any idea of how many miles and hours *that* fact meant? Yes, of course you *could* travel from one to the other, but James knew nothing, but nothing, about 'transportation' between them. Had never visited Charlottesville actually – and didn't want to – it was an intellectual snobs' town. And anyway he wasn't sure that he'd be around on the dates Dan mentioned. He had his commissions to discharge. Could he cancel these? Dan ventured. *Could James cancel them!* What a fucking stupid question! Put it another way – could Dan cancel his conference?

The dogwood was in flower all over Charlottesville; the ambience of the Conference was a peaceful, pleasant one. Dan tried many times to telephone James, but always the number was engaged. (Had his brother left the instrument off the hook?) In their leisure-time Dan and his associates could sit in the gardens of Ash Lawn, the centre of the University and the 'academical village' of Jefferson's own design, proclamatory of his vision of the clearing in the wild, of civilisation established in its most rational form against a background of untilled, untillable mountain-country. With the sky an early summer blue, the neo-classical colonnades a pure white, the brick of the pavilions a mellow red, and the trees a light-filled green, Ash Lawn should have given Dan a sense of near-unadulterated harmony. But instead, just as now in Madrid, he worried about James. Could it be, he asked himself, that in his present commercial man's affluence, and married man's stability, James now despised the eccentricity and shabby-gentility of 'The Cedars' and despised, too, the unromantic, professional class nature of his only brother?

Nevertheless Dan went ahead and bought a Trailways bus ticket to Nashville; he would arrive there early on Saturday morning. He would never forget the journey. Ridge succeeded ridge, all so densely wooded that, upon a summit, Dan felt an inclination to throw himself down upon the tree-tops and bounce upon them as on some natural green trampoline. The judas and dogwood would play upon his face with their fragrant blossoms; and the light which the myriad leaves gave off would cast an envelope about him, and he would desire none other through which to look at the world. THE GREAT STATE OF TENNESSEE a signboard proclaimed, beyond which higher mountains, bathed in the setting sun, rose. Tennessee: James's state! It would be good, no matter what his entrepreneurial disdain led him to say or do, to see his brother again. James's tunes – especially as rendered on the harmonica – filled Dan's head as the bus took him up and down a further prolixity of ridges and seemed at times to be making for the sinking sun itself.

How like a dream the events of the next morning had appeared even at the time! Dan felt sticky and tired after the long night's travel; he was pleased to see at last – like the picture on the sleeve of James's beloved Bob Dylan L.P. – the Nashville skyline, that ugly, jagged consort of skyscrapers upon a hill, quivering in the air of what was obviously going to be a very hot day. On arrival, not even pausing for a wanted coffee at the bus station café, Dan stepped into an air-conditioned taxi and asked to be taken to Scotswood Drive, Building Number 3, apartment 34. The radio of the taxi noisily relayed – appropriately enough – twangy country melodies as it tore through suburbs remarkably like those in Dan's television-inspired, sadly contemptuous imaginings. All was self-protecting luxuriance – architecture, objects, plants. On lawns the sprinklers were already, at this early hour, busy, and families were breakfasting in advertisement-like languor on their mock-classical verandahs, magnolias and tulip trees and judas in flower all round them. Such houses certainly *were* a far cry from 'The Cedars', thought Dan, with Friedrich Mayerhofer's ghastly *tableaux* and the damp kitchen and wonky gate-posts. And then, to Dan's surprise, the taxi exchanged these white, swank homes, these green, umbrous gardens for a dreary roadscape over which heat, uninhibited, danced – a planetoid of flyovers, garages, used-car depots, Pancake Houses, Donut Bars, Exxon Signs, Piggly-Wiggly Stores.

'Scotswood Drive!' announced the taxi-driver, speaking the name over which Dan had speculated for so long, 'here you go!'

But *this* could not be where James lived, this horrible conglomeration of two-storey apartment blocks built of cheap bricks (or substitute bricks) the colour of plums going bad, dumped upon a wasteland in which piles of rubbish and cars like rusty, discarded toys were all too visible? The complex resembled a hideous travesty of an Oxford college. Where velvet lawns existed in the latter, swimming-pools winked back at the harsh sun here; sizzling in coconut oil, girls sprawled beside them, while men in cut-offs and gaudy shirts feasted eyes upon so much indolent flesh. After ascertaining a little agitatedly that he really *was* in the right place, Dan made his way to the door of 34 – James's apartment. It was on the upper storey of one of the more hideous and populous buildings.

Dan knocked upon this door as if carrying out some somnambulistic ritual. No response. God, he'd been stupid to come! Stupid too not to have guessed the reason for James's reluctance. He made himself knock again. And then he heard behind it a stirring, a stumbling within: James, and presumably Cynthia, *were* at home then, to use the strangely inapt phrase.

When the door opened, it did so to reveal a James older-looking than Dan had pictured – but this was not the worst of it. His eyes were very bleary, very blood-shot, his hair as unkempt as a hobo's in a ham movie, his face flushed and covered with at least two days' stubble.

'My God, it's never *you*!' James exclaimed, after a pause which seemed to last hours and in which two pairs of eyes wondered at each other.

Dan could well have exclaimed the same. Instead he said – in an almost pedagogic tone: 'But you *knew* I was in the Southern States, James.'

'Yeah, I did, didn't I?'

'We spoke over the 'phone about it.'

'Yeah, yeah, we did, I recall,' said James, 'but then – see, Dan, I don't react too much to externals these days.'

Indeed he couldn't, for behind him gaped a one-room flat of a near-surreal cheerlessness and mess – clothes and paperbacks strewn all over the floor, a table piled with disgustingly unwashed plates and glasses, and by an unmade double bed a veritable off-licence of bottles, mostly empty: wine, vodka, scotch, bourbon.

'Come right in, Dan,' James bade him, 'make yourself at home!'

It was very ghastly. 'Cynthia?' Dan asked.

'Cynthia?' repeated James, as if he didn't quite understand who Dan was talking about, 'Oh, Cynthia. My little wife; "my wee wifie" as a Scotsman would say. *She*, Dan, had the very good sense to walk out on me ages ago. Can't even figure out when that was from this particular point in Time. Time does pretty strange things to me these days. But I tell you one thing: Cynthia was a real nice girl, but I was mighty glad to see her go. 'Cause her going let me get on with my true business, didn't it?'

'Which is what?' Dan asked fearfully. But he had noticed already – to his relief – James's musical instruments: banjo, guitar, *Hohner* harmonica.

'Being a failure, of course – what else?' James said, 'that's what you'd call my *true* vocation in life, I think.'

'James,' Dan began, but then he saw that his brother had sat down upon the squalid bed – its sheets were stained with spilled red wine, and grimy too – and was in tears.

Dan sat down beside him, and put an arm round him. 'Jamesie, why didn't you tell me how things were with you? About your marriage, about . . .' There was no need to finish. For it was completely obvious that James had no job to call a job, and that all chance of making it in Music City U.S.A. had long ago come to an end.

'I'd thought that becoming a full-time Bluegrass musician was just a matter of playing beautifully,' said James, smiling grimly at him, 'what a fucking fool! For of course it isn't. It's all contracts and who-knows-who, and this deal and that deal, and licking people's asses and all the rest of the crap. *You* probably figured that out from the first.'

Dan hadn't. He'd been as innocent as James.

'Do you do *any* work?' he asked gently.

'Part-time. As a barman in a club.' James gave a wild, mirthless laugh. 'It's not worth talking about, though later we could go to the club and I could fix you a cocktail. Here, Dan, you read books. Ever read *him*?' And he indicated with the toes of his bare dirty left foot a paperback edition of one of Yukio Mishima's novels (then enjoying a posthumous vogue). Others were also there, Dan saw, among the crumpled underpants and screwed-up socks.

'No, I never have.'

'Should do. *He* knew what to do with his life. Went wild and cut his head off! Got a lot of other guys to do the same damn thing too!'

Dan fell back in his fear on English facetiousness: 'Well, I hope you're not going to do that.'

James gave another unstable laugh. 'I haven't got a head left, man,' he said, 'it's another person's, and it's one *full* of *shit*!' He paused. And the very room seemed to Dan fumey with his own horror. 'Want some coffee, Danny-boy? You must be tired after your journey – from where was it now? Charlotte? Charlottesville? Somewhere I've never been to.'

'In a minute, thanks,' said Dan, not bothering to say which of the two towns he had in fact been lecturing in, 'let's talk about things.'

'Let's talk about "The Cedars",' said James, 'how is it? I often imagine myself there – fixing doors, getting the supper ready, pruning the apple trees, painting the outhouses. How's Pappa?'

'Well,' said Dan, 'you'll soon have a chance of finding out. Because you're coming back to England with me. I'll stay here a few days, and will have some money wired out for your ticket.'

And he did, and had. And James had returned. Back to the quiet of life in Tanbury. No hobnobbing with mates or chasing after local girls, though. Instead dedication to Pappa and 'The Cedars', to the trivial round, the common task which apparently he had spent so many hot, empty days in Nashville pining for.

Dan had thought that this life had, all summer and autumn, been healing his brother. Once again he had been proved to be wrong. Six months later James had been admitted into Bencroft after first making a violent attack upon Pappa, then falling into a state of vacancy that resembled catalepsy. And yet during that August, September, early October he *had* seemed at peace; he had been resourceful about the house and garden, and had played his harmonica with exceptional (even by *his* standards) tenderness. And he had been able to inspire love in young, mixed-up Kevin. So what had gone wrong?

If Dan traced Kevin to some gay lair tonight, he might find out.

PART THREE

I

Kevin's day had followed the course he'd assigned to it. Now, at a late hour by English standards, he stood in the underground room of the gay club he most frequented. Very many boys were dancing, though not so much with, as at, each other. The busy stroboscopic lighting made torsoes, crutches, thighs appear to be continuously alighting and pausing in mid-air, detached from their dithyrambic owners, like luminous birds on the wing. Kevin, however, was not one of those dancing; he was in the shadows, leaning against the bar. Behind him a youngish man, with brilliantly henna'ed hair, and dangling, glistening ear-rings, was serving drinks, and at his side two youths, locked in a tight embrace, enjoyed each other with restless mouths and hands.

Round his forehead Kevin had tied, Miguel Bosé-style, his favourite handkerchief, white but patterned with blue and black flowers. A beam of light from the central part of the room picked this out so that it resembled, or so Kevin imagined, some halo of the flesh. All evening boys and older men had been looking at him admiringly, often trying to beckon him away from where he stood – on to the dance-floor, into corners, even towards the *servicio* (lavatory). But Kevin had taken no notice of any of them; he had preferred to stare into his golden-brown whisky and remember how James Varney used to sing to his banjo in his gruff voice:

'If the river was whisky and I a duck,
        I'd dive to the bottom and never come up . . .'

In America James had, he'd once confessed, found solace in whisky when despair descended on him. When he'd made the confession it had been hard to imagine him in despair. Now it was hard to imagine him in any other condition.

A number of Kevin's friends were at the club tonight – Nolo and Paco, his lunch-mates, and on the floor now he could watch Juan and Nano and Jaime dancing, seemingly intoxicated by their own movements. How well Kevin knew the routines they were putting themselves through so that the evening could come to a gratifying, and possibly lucrative, ending. But he didn't feel up to any of that tonight; Dan's embraces were still young and green in his mind. He thrust a hand into his left-hand pocket, and felt an abundance of coins – of *duros*, of 25 and 50 peseta pieces. Yes, quite enough for what he wanted. Taking his half-drained glass with him, he edged a difficult way to the telephone cubicle which stood to the left of the *servicio* door. He'd often used this 'phone before, there being no instrument in the house in the Calle de San Marcos.

07 produced the high, pauseless dialling tone for abroad. Then 44 brought you to Britain – after which your fingers worked the individual number you wanted. It was odd how automatically they did this tonight; it must have been eight months at least since last they'd done so. The familiar burr-burr, burr-burr of the London telephone ringing out suddenly made the city itself seem peculiarly near; Kevin felt for a moment that the place had shrunk to Lilliputian proportions and he could lean a listening head against it.

'Hullo!' The voice was faint and identityless.

'May I speak to Jason Fletcher, please?' Saliva left his mouth; indeed his whole head felt suddenly light and dry.

'This *is* Jason Fletcher,' said the voice, now as loud and clear as if it were indeed proceeding from a shrunken city only inches away from Kevin.

'Jason, it's Kevin here, Kevin Lalland!' As if he could be any other!

'Kevin? Christ, what a surprise! Where are you? In this world or the next?'

'In this one,' said Kevin, thinking how soon with Jason you fell into facetious banter.

'I have my doubts but I'll believe you. Which particular part of it are you in?'

'Madrid. Still.'

'Yes, that's where your parents said you were. I contacted them,

you see; I was worried about where you might have taken yourself
off to and what you might be doing.'

Kevin made a resolution to steel himself against being touched
by such words from Jason. Nevertheless, he thought – that's exactly
what Jason *would* have done. And of how many others would that
be true – particularly after receiving vitriolic, hysterical abuse both
from the mouth and from the pen? But Jason was continuing:

'Your parents had a sort of P.O. Box number for you. I thought all
that very cloak-and-daggerish, as if you were gun-running for the
Carlists. I began several letters to you, then decided you wouldn't
want to hear from me. I expect I was right?' There was a pleading
note in Jason's voice.

Kevin didn't know how to answer him. Would he have liked a
letter? On the whole, for all his waves of hatred, perhaps yes.

'So you're happy in your Madrid life, Kevin?'

'I suppose so.' 'Happy' would be an odd word for his feelings,
Kevin thought.

'Look, all this must be costing you a lot. It'd be better if *I* rang
you – I'm well-off after all, enmeshed in my evil world of the
media, as you once put it. Give me your number and I'll call you
straight back.'

Kevin could not but remember now all the many kindnesses
he had had in his time from Jason at *Project*. He said: 'That's really
very good of you. I'd appreciate it.' And he gave him the club's
number.

Turning round he now saw, standing rather too close to the
'phone cubicle, a brawny, bearded man in the now fashionable pale
yellow sweater and brown corduroy trousers. He was, Kevin esti-
mated, in his late thirties, the same age as Daniel Varney, to whom
in fact – beard apart – he bore a slight resemblance. And not only
in appearance; Kevin saw that he too was 'taken' with him, was
preparing to introduce himself. But I don't want him or anyone
else right now, said Kevin, memories of last night's love-making
once again hallucinatorily vivid in his mind's eye. He turned his
back on this intent-expressioned bloke, and stared at the white
telephone, with his gaze imploring it to ring, and immediately.
How long would it/could it take for Jason to obtain this Madrid
number? He tried to remember what law of the physical universe

telephone calls entailed, and as he was trying to do so – without success; he'd failed 'O' level Physics! – the 'phone sounded.

'Hullo!'

'That you, Kevin?'

'Yes, it's me. Thanks for ringing back. It's really good of you.' He was speaking exactly as he had done in the old days when he'd worked at *Project* and Jason had given him a cup of coffee, an interesting assignment, an afternoon off.

'It's so amazing that I've been given the opportunity of doing so. Is it your Madrid flat I'm ringing?'

'Jason, how do you imagine I could afford a flat – in Madrid, or anywhere? I live in a little room at the top of a house – it'd make your blood run cold just to hear it described. And it's certainly got no telephone. No, I'm ringing from a club.'

'What kind of club?' Jason was probably picturing him in the Madrid 'White Elephant Club' or at any rate in some smart journalists' hang-out.

'What kind do you think?' he answered pointedly.

There was a brief pause. During it words came back to Kevin from the past. They were sitting, Jason and he, in a smoky, oak-panelled pub off Fleet Street. 'I won't make any bones about it,' Jason was saying, 'I do find you sexually attractive, Kevin, and I suppose I have done ever since you first started at *Project*. Maybe that's why I've become so friendly with you. But it stops at *feeling*, and you must get that firmly into your head. There can be no, *no* question of anything else.' He'd sounded so bloody pleased at his own forthrightness.

Wouldn't the speech have been more palatable if he hadn't admitted to the attraction?

. . . 'Actually,' Jason was continuing, 'you're lucky to have got me at the flat. Early tomorrow morning Sorrel and I are leaving for Tanbury where, between us, we've bought a house.'

'In *Tanbury!*' exclaimed Kevin, and, in a kaleidoscope more whirring and multi-coloured than any club lights, he saw St. Jude's Vicarage, the market square and cross; he saw too 'The Cedars' and, standing in its garden, James Varney with his hands cupped round his harmonica.

'There's no need to be quite so astonished; it *was* the scene of my adolescence after all. As a matter of fact we've . . .' And he stopped in mid-sentence, obviously not wishing to continue to the end. 'I shall be keeping on a rented London flat, of course,' he went on after this hiatus, speaking fast and a little self-importantly, 'it would be impossible to commute every day to London from Oxfordshire. Anyway, enough of all my domestic arrangements. I want to know how *you* are, Kevin.' And he sounded as if he really did. As was almost certainly the case; Jason was never lacking in curiosity.

'I'm okay.'

'But what are you *doing* with yourself – apart from going to gay bars?'

Precious little else, Kevin almost replied. 'It's hard to give an account of my life over the telephone,' he said, 'but,' he added a little proudly, 'I've learned Spanish.' This might or might not impress Jason who spoke and read several languages with energetic fluency.

'I often think about you, you know, Kevin.'

I must *not* succumb to his charms, Kevin told himself. Aloud he said: 'Maybe you do, but then I expect there are many times when you don't, and wouldn't want to. When you're with Sorrel, for instance.'

In the seconds before Jason replied, the disco music from the club's main underground room surged forth louder than ever: 'I Just Can Get Enough. I Just Can Get Enough'. Then – 'I thought that sort of remark belonged firmly to the past,' Jason said, 'and you must know, Kevin, that Sorrel and I got married some months back. That was one of the things I wanted to write to you about.'

Married – well, it had to come to that some day, thought Kevin. Sorrel was a nice, a good person with a gentle, imaginative manner. All the same, *married*! London, which all day he'd been missing as never before, and with an intensity that he'd not thought possible, now seemed to slip away from him; the Lilliputian city was being snatched up by Gulliver's hands. Meetings with Jason could never be the same now. But – 'Congratulations!' he said lamely.

'Thank you,' said Jason, clearly registering the lameness, 'and now may I ask if you had any special reason for ringing me up, or was it just as a result of some stab of morbid curiosity?'

Kevin had almost forgotten Jason's capacity for the cruel *mot juste.* James Varney would not have forgotten this, however. 'No,' he said, 'I wanted to ask you something. Yesterday night in the Paseo de Recoletos (that's, I suppose, Madrid's main avenue) I met someone you must know.'

'Really? Who?'

'Daniel Varney.'

'So,' said Jason, 'we're still travelling along the same track? Still obsessed by the Varneys? Did you *really* meet him, Kevin, or is this some trick?'

'Of course it isn't a trick,' Kevin all but shouted, greatly to the interest of the still-watching bearded man, 'but now you'll probably think I'm suffering from delusions, that I've gone quite *loco* like poor old James.' Let that shaft go home, he said to himself.

Jason's tone, when he replied, was indeed gentle again, conciliatory:

'Okay, I've done you an injustice. You *did* meet him. But what am I supposed to do about it? Did my name come up at all?'

'Not exactly,' Kevin hedged, 'tell me what he's like?'

'Is *that* what you've rung up about? Why can't you find out for yourself if you've met him.'

'It was an inconclusive sort of meeting last night,' Kevin answered uneasily; he had not anticipated this particular probing, 'and I'm not sure when I'll be seeing him again' – if ever, he added sadly to himself – 'but I liked him; it would be good to know more about him.'

'Oh, I think I can understand what sort of meeting it was; I've guessed for some years that Dan is that way,' said Jason, and, of course, he would: he was so bloody quick off the mark where sexual matters were concerned. 'Well, what can I tell you about him that would be of any help? I *was* a very close friend of his; then things came between us. Things? James, your hero! I liked Dan, he was always an independent sort of person, lonely, not all that easy to know, easily moved by the plight of the underdog. Like me.' Oh, yeah, thought Kevin, though, of course, it *was* true that much of Jason's working life – at *Project*, in his articles for the Sundays, in his scripts for TV – concerned itself with that category of mankind: gipsies, squatters, lesbians, junkies, mostly, however, as reflected

in one art-form or another. 'But even as a boy, Dan's main love
was . . .' But once again, as when talking about his own new house
in Tanbury, he dropped the sentence, as if afraid of it. This time,
though, Kevin decided that he must be made to finish it.

'Is *what* – or *who*?' After only one night it was odd to mind so
much about the answer.

'Is James,' said Jason, 'I don't think I've encountered a case of
an elder brother being so deeply bound up with a younger one.
Perhaps it was because they were so cooped together in that awful,
batty atmosphere of "The Cedars". Even though Dan was so much
cleverer and more sensible than James, I swear he *looked up to him*.
Don't ask me for what. Ask yourself! You also seem to have done
so.'

'Yes, Jason, I did,' said Kevin.

'But why, *why*?' said Jason. 'Try to put James Varney once and
for all out of your head, Kevin. For one thing he probably thinks
gay folk like you ought to be ridden out of town on a rail. For
another he can have no part to play in your life at all now, even
though you may have met up for a giddy night with his brother. I
suppose you're feeling guilty and angry about . . . about the business of this time last year. As I said then, *often*, there's no need to.
It's all quite irrational on your part. Any amends there are to make,
I will make – in fact I've tried already. Now that you've learned
Spanish, you'd be far, *far* better employed trying to find out all you
can about the culture of an *extremely* interesting and potentially
important country.' This last sentence was spoken in the tone he
used at editorial meetings – how it brought back memories of the
Board Room at *Project*, with himself too shy to speak, and prefer-
ring, when not listening to or watching Jason and all the others, to
let his gaze travel over the walls and roofs of the red brick Victorian piles of surrounding Clerkenwell.

'I suppose you're right,' said Kevin. Though, if in a restricted
way, he *had* found out quite a lot about Spain already.

'As *I'm* paying for this call,' said Jason, 'is it possible to get you
to inquire after me? How I'm doing, what I've been writing, how
I'm feeling about this or that? No, I suppose such matters wouldn't
interest you very much.'

You tended to forget that Jason Fletcher had feelings, real feelings. Kevin said: 'Oh, Jason, of *course* such matters interest me. Though actually . . .' this time it was Kevin who didn't want to finish a sentence. But he did. 'Actually if you were to tell me about your doings, I'd probably want to come straight back to England.'

'Then why don't you, you silly nerd? What do you want to hide yourself away in Madrid for?'

'You know why,' said Kevin, 'because, as you said, I'm still feeling guilty and angry. Sometimes, as I walk about the Madrid Calles, the idea comes to me that I am a murderer. The only one in sight!'

'With me as an accomplice, I suppose,' said Jason, 'or perhaps rather the director of operations. The Godfather!'

Kevin made no reply. For this *was* how he thought, and why deny it? After a pause he went on, knowing that his voice was becoming a little hysterical – and audible to others in the club. '*You* know – though James never will – that I'd heard him play the harmonica in the garden of "The Cedars" at least a week *before* you gave me the "commission" and suggested I got to know him. I didn't guess what you were going to do. Are you still there, Jason?' But he didn't wait for assurance. 'I didn't guess that you'd drive a father into the grave and a son into the madhouse.' And me into all kinds of hells, he could have added!

'Kevin,' Jason's voice was its most patience-timbred, 'you know as well as I do that that's a very jaundiced and unjust account of what happened. We've been through all this before.'

'Oh, yes,' said Kevin with tearful sarcasm, 'we've been through all this before. The humanist journalist has explained everything!' Then, most likely undoing the (intendedly) stinging effect of this, Kevin went on in a more piteous tone: 'And last night – yes, I slept with him, as you've guessed – I took to Dan *so* much. Perhaps he's the man I've been looking for all these years. But I can't see him again! How could I? – his only family's murderer!'

'Kevin!' Jason protested.

'I'd have liked to go back to England with him,' Kevin said, 'oh, yes, I'm really fond of Madrid and feel at home here. But after last night . . . I want to be back in England. I'd even,' Oh, Christ, he mustn't start crying, 'I'd even like to see *you* again. I'd like things to be as they used to be between us.'

'And so would I, Kevin,' Jason said, with unmistakable sincerity, 'so would I! I might even be able to assist you back to a job, not on *Project*, of course,' he added, almost hastily, ' – and, of course, jobs of any kind are very hard to get in Maggie Thatcher's Right Little England, but . . .'

Jason always covered himself in that sort of way. A job on a respectable English magazine – how far away from Kevin's present life that was!

'Kevin, you there?' it was Jason's turn to ask, but not trusting himself to speak further, Kevin replaced the receiver.

Yes, fuck it, how many good things as well as bad there could be to think about Jason, his most cherished enemy.

And now his interested watcher was stepping out of his shadows to address him – in Spanish. (No, he didn't, closer to, look at all like Dan Varney!) Might he be so bold as to say that, for him, Kevin was the best-looking boy in the place. He hadn't been able to take his eyes off him all the time he was telephoning. (Had he been calling a lover perhaps? He'd sounded so very emotional, so *un*-English!) Anyway, he would like to buy Kevin a drink at the bar, while quenching his *own* thirst – a thirst for proper knowledge of him.

Kevin had schooled himself so long into accepting such proposals that he did not refuse. Presently he was holding his second glass of whisky that night – he'd drained the first during his 'phone call – while the man stood by, watching him as a trapper might some newly caught animal.

His name, he said, was Isidro, and he was a lawyer in Burgos. He did not often come into Madrid, but when he did, *here* was his favourite haunt. And yet today he'd not been able to enter the bar or disco-dancing area, so mesmerised had he been by Kevin's delicious appearance as he stood by the 'phone. And might he venture to hope that his own appearance was not altogether distasteful to Kevin? At this point he took out of his pocket an absurd pair of tinted spectacles which he put on with a dandyish gesture. Then he leered.

Kevin had probably guessed, he continued, the reason why he was in Madrid this Sunday. Today's demonstrations could surely be accounted a great success, such near-tangible enthusiasm, such – if he may use the word – spirituality. No doubt the liberal press – *El Pais* above all – would see fit to belittle its significance; no doubt

Calvo Sotelo's wretched, perpetually compromising government would speak of it with nervous disapproval. For him, however, it had been a day that he would remember for ever, a day in which he would always be proud to have been a participant.

He may be wrong (his body was touching Kevin's at several points now) but he felt Kevin, foreigner though he was, was a sympathiser to The Cause. Strength, that was what he, Isidro, respected above all. Without strength, where were you? Spain was fragmented now, because its government had abandoned ideals for pragmatic comforts: she needed to be healed, united, made *strong* and *one* again – and through palpable Might – embodied in the Church, the Army, the Police, in trained youth and obedient girls. He wiped his brow, talking thus obviously excited him. Behind his strawberry-coloured lenses his eyes were darting here, there and everywhere – appraising Kevin's face and body, the hair visible on the barman's chest, the Dionysian youths.

Yes, he knew what Kevin was going to say next: in the Franco era, in the pre-democratic days, life hadn't been so easy for gays. (Kevin, in point of fact, had given no indication of being about to say anything, and 'next' was an inappropriate word since he'd hardly spoken during the whole encounter.) Well, that *was* indeed a point, but it need not affect one's dislike of democracy or one's belief in the necessity and beauty of Force.

For after all wasn't there something paradoxical – he now adjusted his glasses, sipped the tonic-water he'd bought for himself, and gave Kevin another elegant smirk – in homosexuals, who constituted a minority, an *élite*, if you liked, championing the system which upheld the will of the *majority*, of the mindless rabble – i.e. democracy? Nor was this the only reason for a gay to be a Franquista: think of the masculine beauty of the fighting life!

'You have almost finished your drink, I see. Let me get you another. A "chaser", as you call it in your language,' Isidro sniggered into his beard. 'I'm sure this drink is going to be the beginning of a mutually satisfying friendship.'

Kevin had been horrified by Isidro's words, at once so cruel and complacent. The best person at dealing with such evil-minded nonsense would have been the man he'd just been talking to. Indeed his abilities in this direction had earned him what reputation he enjoyed. Kevin concentrated internally upon his former friend and boss, and aloud said:

'And I'm equally sure it's going to be nothing of the kind. How *could* I be friendly with someone who thinks as you do? Why,' and he pulled a hundred-peseta note out of his pocket, 'I don't want so much as to have accepted a drink from you.' And he cast the paper money upon the bar counter.

Isidro's smile broadened . . .

Kevin made as if to leave the club. But he had got no further than the *servicio* door when he saw coming down the stairs towards him two men . . .

'No,' Richard had said, at the entrance to the club in the dingy street with jutting eaves, 'we're not much like Dante and Virgil; you were right, I was wrong!'

'This is the club which young people gravitate to,' said Dan, 'or so the Gay Guide says, and so there really is a good chance of his being here.'

'It's a real mystery to me how you can bear so much as to enter such places,' Richard said, 'so much hunger of the flesh proclaimed so publicly. Don't you find something a *little* obscene about the whole business? It's like being transported into a canvas by Hieronymus Bosch.'

'There must have been a time when I did,' said Dan, 'but it's too long ago now for me to recapture it properly. There was a time too, I must tell you, when I found gay clubs extremely exciting. Now I just take them for granted – as places where you can encounter those with the same sexual inclination as yourself. And that isn't so very awful, is it?'

'So you've arrived at an "autumnal" approach,' said Richard, not answering the last question, 'all right, then – in we go. But I warn you, this is the last establishment I visit, Danny. I want to go back to my *hostal* – to finish unpacking, and to read then a few pages of *The Hound of the Baskervilles.*'

'*The Hound of the Baskervilles?*' said Dan, as they pushed open a commissionaire-guarded door and beheld a long dark room where cocktails were being served and various male couples were sitting in intimate attitudes on plush sofas.

'Sherlock Holmes, Father Brown, Miss Marple – I'd give away Hamlet and Lear and Othello for their company, as I believe I must have told you before, and certainly for all the gay joints in the *world*. Lumme, Dan, this place is the worst of all; make this visit *short!*'

'Downstairs seems to be where the action is,' Dan said.

'It's certainly where the hideous music is,' said Richard. As he followed Dan down the tortuous staircase on which youths were standing in sexy poses, he wondered why he hadn't as yet been able to tell Dan that piece of Tanbury gossip – that the elderly man who'd bought 'The Cedars' from Dan after Hampton Varney's death having himself died, the house had been re-sold and its present owner was of all people, Jason Fletcher. Just as he was pondering exactly what Dan's reaction to this would or could be, he felt his arm gripped. 'Ricky, he's here! I knew it! – you see the search wasn't the madcap idea you thought it was. I've been vindicated.'

And all this for some tarmac cowboy, Richard thought. But that was to forget, of course, the harmonica and the connection with James, James who obsessed Dan so. 'Which is he?' he began to ask, but the question was soon rendered redundant – Dan let go of him and went up to embrace a slim young man with large dark eyes and curly hair and an expression of soulful pertness on his face. Across his brow there wound a scarf like some luminous serpent.

'I thought we'd *never* meet again,' this young man was saying.

'And you did your best to see that we wouldn't!' Dan replied.

'If you knew why,' Kevin said, 'you wouldn't be surprised at my behaviour. You see, I wanted to spare us both pain.'

Dan gazed into the boy's eyes as an ornithologist might look upon the head of a precious, rare bird that he had finally traced to its remote nest – with wonder, gratitude, exhaustion. 'It's *so* good to see you, Kevin,' he said, 'last night when I discovered you weren't there, in my room, any longer, I . . .' He seemed unable to describe his emotion.

'Yes, I did things the wrong way,' said Kevin, 'but then I usually do, don't I? And me, I'm pleased too. That you tracked me down. Because that's what you *have* done, isn't it? Not that it can have been very difficult. It's never difficult to track down a whore.'

Dan pulled the boy very close to him. This act of affectionate supplication was not, in fact, incongruous in this club, so many were its claspings and huggings. But wherever it had taken place, its obvious, blazing sincerity would have impressed, Richard thought: yes, wherever you'd seen it, it would have been the surroundings that were humbled.

'Please don't speak like that; you mustn't,' Dan was saying, 'for one thing it doesn't become you. And you really needn't have worried so much about sparing me pain. *James* is behind this – isn't he? – and goodness, what a lot of pain I've known on his behalf.'

'But there are many, many things you *don't* know, Dan,' said Kevin, 'and,' he gave a tragic little smile, 'none of them is going to make you like me any the more.'

'Like, dislike,' said Dan, 'they aren't so affected by knowledge as we often think. Don't be afraid, Kevin. Don't be afraid, Paseo harmonica-player!'

'But you don't even know who I am,' Kevin protested. Tears were welling in his eyes.

'I think I do,' said Dan, 'I worked it out, a short while back, while remembering episodes from my Tanbury past. You're Kevin Lalland – nephew of my father's old friends, Edward and Frances Lalland.'

'Well, on this Stanley-Livingstone note, I think I'll leave you both,' said Richard, 'Sherlock Holmes and bed summon me. I'll call round at your hotel for breakfast tomorrow morning, Dan. I hope your night is not too *bouleversant!*'

2

When, after a long climb up steep stairs, they reached the top storey of the building in the Calle de San Marcos, Dan had to follow Kevin down unlit corridors and was reminded of nothing so much as that visit to James's apartment, eighteen months ago, in that dreadful sun-soaked, dirty-plum-coloured block in Nashville, Tennessee. How could so many people be accommodated up here, underneath the tiles, he wondered, close, it seemed, to the very stars? Not that there were many signs of life. Behind most doors all was silent and dark.

Anyway here he was at No. 16 – and as Kevin opened the door for him with a mock bow, Dan again thought of his Nashville experience. 'Welcome,' Kevin said, 'welcome to No. 16, Sexta Planta; 40, Calle de San Marcos! Welcome to my humble home!'

Not, humble though it undoubtedly was, and dreary, that it was sordid as James's had been. It was clean, attempts had been made at personalising it, and there was a pervading smell of patchouli.

'*Nice*, isn't it?' Kevin said, giving just such a truculent smile as he'd bestowed on Dan back in the Recoletos last night. Indeed his cheeky manner had returned, perhaps out of embarrassment at showing someone where he lived. 'I'm so glad to have the opportunity of entertaining you here! Sit you down, please – you actually have a choice of chair, and then there's also the bed. *Single* only, I'm sorry to say! We can eat, drink and be merry, can't we? While I spill my terrible beans. I have a few tea-bags, and some rather stale *madelenas* – they're a kind of dry Spanish sponge-cake,' he added, by way of explanation.

'Just tea would be fine,' Dan said, 'I had a sizable dinner with Richard at a *mesón* near the Plaza Mayor.'

'Richard, that was your friend?'

'Yes,' said Dan, 'a very good friend too.'

'Funny bloke, I thought. The *Viznaga* wasn't exactly his scene, was it? He behaved rather as if he'd landed behind the glass in the snake house at London Zoo.'

'Perhaps,' said Dan wryly, 'it's we who are funny!' What was that shape covered by a blue cloth in front of the window? he wondered.

Kevin pointed at the posters of Miguel Bosé and David Bowie. 'That kind of talk isn't allowed here,' he said. Then, his expression and voice changing, he said, 'Not that, considering what I've got to reveal to you, I've any right to tell you what to say and not to say.'

'Is it so very terrible?' asked Dan, but he asked the conventionally assuring question seriously.

'You may,' said Kevin, 'after you've heard me out, want to *kill* me!' There was a decided hysterical edge to his voice, one the ordinary world likes to call 'girlish', though, as Dan, the speech-consultant, knew very well, girls never sound so.

'That's not likely,' said Dan, 'I've never wanted to kill anybody, and don't think I'll make a beginning with *you*. But I think it'd be better for both of us if you started your story now. Procrastination only makes matters worse.'

Despite this advice, Kevin took his time over making tea for the two of them (he boiled water in an old saucepan, and then dropped tea-bags into it; he had no kettle). Dan found himself thinking – for all the similarities that doubtless inhabited the caverns of their two beings – how different he at twenty-four had been from Kevin now. He'd never positioned himself on a gay promenade in advertising red sweater and socks, he'd never haunted pick-up bars. Instead serious conversations with Richard, punctuated with innocent jokes, evenings of music on the gramophone and in concert halls: Haydn and Beethoven quartets, Schubert and Schumann lieder . . .

Then, emptying a heaped teaspoonful of sugar into Dan's mug, Kevin, in a tremulous voice, said: 'I liked your brother more than anyone I've ever met. You must realise that.'

'Well,' said Dan, taken aback by both the suddenness and the directness of this statement, 'I can understand that; he *is* very nice.' *Nice?* What an odd choice of word for James. 'You know, I take it,' he asked diffidently, 'about James *now?*'

'Obviously,' said Kevin, 'you see, Dan,' he brandished a plate of the stale *madelenas* almost wildly at him, 'it was me who *caused* him to be where he is!'

'But that couldn't possibly be true!' Dan protested. For who had been more closely concerned with James's admission to Bencroft than himself?

'But I tell you, it is!' said Kevin.

In a flash of memory Dan held Kevin in his arms last night, felt his cock stiff against his own, his sweet-tasting tongue in his mouth. And these delights, he reflected, had been given him by someone who knew secrets about the worst hours of the person who meant more to him than anyone else.

'That article,' Kevin was saying, 'you remember that *Observer* article?'

'How could I not!' said Dan, 'I was thinking about it only today. It appeared exactly a year ago.' And life has never been the same since, he could have added.

'That fact hadn't escaped me either,' said Kevin, with a crooked

smile, 'it did terrible damage to James didn't it? Well, you can blame
that on . . . on your pretty-boy of last night.'

'I just don't see how,' began Dan uncertainly. But why protest,
he asked himself, *he* was speaking from ignorance where presumably Kevin had knowledge. Underneath that blue cloth there's a
bird-cage, he realised irrelevantly, and inside, isn't there a canary,
asleep on a perch? But perhaps it wasn't all that irrelevant, for he
felt caged like some bird in this room and in this hour, destined to
hear things that could only distress him, even if they shed light on
what had hitherto remained dark.

Stumbling over sentences Kevin started with a brief account of
his home-life. Prosperous and bleak, as Dan had, from the first,
surmised. He had, of course, met, if briefly, Kevin's father, but he
didn't let on about this. He hadn't cared for the man with his lan-
guid manner and his complaisantly worn *ennui*. But then neither,
it appeared, did Kevin. 'I can't remember not feeling a disappointment to my parents,' he said, 'I am their only child, you see, and
not at all what they wanted. From a young age I was too . . . ,' and
he turned tense, pleading eyes upon Dan again, just as patients
were wont to, 'too *effeminate* for their tastes.' He all but shouted
the pejorative adjective; clearly it cost him a lot to speak it aloud.
But that shouldn't surprise; it was one thing for his behaviour to
strive after effeminacy, quite another for him to pronounce the syllables of the quality as pertinent to his whole self, past and present. Kevin then went on to describe the need for the respect and
affection denied him at home that had led him to make so many
experiments in relations, and which he'd felt had been assuaged
for the first time in his friendship with his first boss, Jason Fletcher.
'And I haven't got to ask you whether you know *him*, have I?' he
said.

Indeed he hadn't, but Dan, perhaps stupidly, had by no means
anticipated Jason's entry into the history. But now it had been
made, it seemed totally inevitable. That fight between Jason and
James on that long-ago May day had ended *nothing*, had it? just as
Richard had said, however much at the time it might seem to have
done. For Dan – and for James – the world still rocked because of
the latter's wounded pride and incredulous fury.

'After leaving art-school, I trundled my portfolio round to every

publisher and magazine I could think of; I showed them my drawings of gay young boys juxtaposed with lizards and crickets and
swollen bees, and my designs for imaginary L.P.s. by David Bowie
and Elton John. And they all said – "You *do* appreciate how bad a
time this is to be flogging your work, don't you? If you only knew
how many people I see with folders full of stuff like yours." Only a
pick-up at "The Coleherne" or "The Salisbury" could console me
after some of the snubs I received. Instead of a simple goodbye, the
Art Editor, or whoever it was, would take good care to wound. To
see that I didn't come back, I suppose . . . And then I went to *Project*
where there was a job on offer and was interviewed by Jason and
another man. Jason was so different from his counterparts at other
places – amiable, interested, even then full of quips and personal
questions.'

Yes, Dan could imagine that. He'd always aroused the gratitude and admiration of younger boys at school, and with his own
brothers had been tenderly, unoppressively attentive.

'Well, I was given the job, and God knows I worked hard enough
to repay Jason's kindness for his advocacy of me over other candi-
dates. Jason became, I suppose, a sort of obsession with me. I'd
never leave the office before he did, I'd bring him little presents –
well, some of them, not so little – and I'd pay him fulsome compliments . . .'

'Were you in love with him?' Dan asked. He had never been –
there were too many sharp edges to Jason.

'No, I don't think so. Well, perhaps a little.' He blushed. 'I'd have
done anything he wanted me to.'

He then added: 'But there was absolutely no question of him
asking me to do the things that I suppose *I* most wanted. He himself made that quite plain.' He was clearly tempted to qualify these
remarks, then decided not to.

'I can never forget also how kind Jason was to me on a late
August day last year. I'd got out of bed that morning to find that
when I rested my weight upon my feet, it was as if a knife were
being mercilessly twisted into my body. Four hours later, in Jason's
office at *Project*, as he discussed illustrations for an article on the
East German Theatre, that knife was still attacking me – whenever
I moved suddenly, whenever I got up from a chair or sat down on

one, whenever I took a deep breath. "Kevin, whatever's the matter with you?" Jason said. "You look in a dreadful way. As white as a . . . I can't do anything better than 'sheet'."

'I *felt* like a sheet, like a shroud. Jason insisted not only that I went back home to Lewisham, but that he escorted me. He even waited to hear what the doctor diagnosed. Which was pleurisy.

'I know I'm talking to a doctor right now, but in my opinion it was all the frustrations of my life that brought me pleurisy: unrequited feelings for Jason; promiscuity outside home, childlike irresponsibility within it; people not appreciating my artwork. For two whole days I was delirious with a high fever; lying in bed was like being on a ship that some burning, lurid-coloured sea was tossing. I had the sensation of passing islands where I could have felt better and of not being allowed to land on them by some malign force. When the fever subsided, I felt more exhausted than I could ever remember feeling before. I could not even find the energy for reading or listening to the wireless; instead I went over and over my past. Particularly my recent past. Sometimes it seemed so unmitigatedly unsatisfactory that I wanted to fall back into delirium again. But I didn't – or *couldn't*! I made a vow that I would begin to live more honestly, that I would make a clean breast of everything to my parents.'

'You mean about sex?' said Dan.

'Yes, that above all else. It was hard.'

'I can imagine!' said Dan. He could picture the disdain on Gerald Lalland's jowly, handsome, unsympathetic face.

'Did *you* ever do it?' asked Kevin, almost eagerly. He clearly wanted to establish another link before the grim part of his narrative began.

'No!' said Dan. For Mamma had died before any confession was really necessary, and as for Pappa, it was impossible to imagine a conversation with him on any intimate matter. For him Dan had moved through life swathed in moral virtue, and that was that!

'That confession's not something I'd go through again. I didn't do it very well either – I giggled too much, and in the wrong places, and was too full of apologies and little pleas. I also told my parents far more than was necessary. One always does in such cases . . . Still I suppose it could have gone even worse.'

Gerald Lalland, Dan conjectured, would have helped himself to a stiff, double scotch-on-the-rocks; 'Mummy,' fluttery, would have silently prayed that the whole conversation could be cancelled.

'Actually,' Kevin went on, 'they made very few *direct* comments on the subject. What they *did* say was that I was clearly in need of a break, and that the doctor had already recommended them to send me out of London for a good rest. They got *Project* to give me sick-leave, and off I went to stay with my Uncle Edward and my Aunt Frances in Tanbury. I had not stayed there for some time, my father having little in common with his brother and sister.' ('Tanbury's a tedious place,' Dan heard Gerald's voice saying.) 'St. Jude's Vicarage seemed to me innocent beyond all words, not really my sort of ambience at all. My bedroom,' smiled Kevin, 'had old prints of animals on the walls, and samplers too – in fact the entire house is *full* of samplers – and there was a patchwork quilt on the bed and lots of Victorian and Edwardian children's books on the shelves. I read *The Story of a Red Deer* and all E. Nesbit's stories about the Psammead and the Phoenix and *The Secret Garden*. Aunt Frances was busy with corn-dollies – over which I was a great help, let me tell you! Uncle Edward was a bit over-persistent in his attempts to interest me in ritual – by which apparently I'd been fascinated when I was a small boy – and I got to dread the sight of an odd little book called *The Ritual Reason Why* . . . Still I made up for my lack of Anglo-Catholic devotion by my enthusiasm for his garden and the "baggy-trousered" chickens.'

At this point both Dan and Kevin laughed – and what a contrast the subject of their laughter was to the *Viznaga* or this room in the Calle de San Marcos. Dan realised that their laughter partook of the nature of a punctuation mark, a caesura. 'And what about Tanbury itself?' Dan asked.

'Well, I'm a real city boy, aren't I?' Kevin said. And from what he knew of him – his familiarity with the *Gijón*, with Chueca and its plenitude of gay bars, his delight in the hobos and down-and-outs to be seen on the streets and at the Metro entrances – Dan could not dispute this. 'For one thing it seemed to me odd to be in a place you could walk completely out of in ten minutes flat. And in one without a single homosexual club, or proper cinema and with only two bookshops, neither much good. But I was determined to be happier than I'd been in recent months, and so I followed my uncle's advice of going for long solitary walks.

'September last year was very beautiful – well, you must remember it, though I don't think you visited Tanbury then, did you? Or rather I never heard of your doing so. A golden haze hung almost perpetually over the town and the countryside – in fact I sometimes had the feeling that the fields were giving it off, releasing light back to the sky. They were cutting the corn in the farmland, the apples were ripening in all the orchards, and there were nuts and plump blackberries in the hedgerows. It was as if I were seeing these trees and fruits and flowers for the first time in my life, as perhaps in a real sense I was. By the end of my first week in Tanbury – for all the stabs of loneliness I had from time to time – London, *Project*, "The Coleherne" and my austere home in Lewisham came to seem, well . . . strangely distant to me.'

Dan thought of his own youthful country walks, when, simultaneous with his delight in all growing things and in prospects of Cotswold hills or Northamptonshire plain, had been relentless fantasies for a life very different from any Tanbury and its environs could offer. He'd imagined breakthroughs he would make in psycho-linguistics, concerts he would attend of advanced chamber or instrumental music, male lovers he would be at last free to enjoy. He'd imagined an absence of the prying, censorious faces of the town's snobbish middle class, and a release from hearing Pappa boom on about Shakespeare's mantle and England's hidden Teutonic mythology (re-found, it would seem, by himself) and the day when Time's great Wheel would fully have turned, and 'my books will be needed again'.

'On the evening of my fifth day in Tanbury,' said Kevin, 'I went for a walk up the road that runs past *your* house, "The Cedars", to get a view of both the Cotswolds to the west and the Midlands plain to the north. I stopped – very near your gate, but on the other side of the road – and looked ahead of me, to gaze upon the silvery-gold light rising from the patchwork of fields up into the deepening sky. I suddenly knew tranquillity. And knew too that I'd never known it before. And then, as if to confirm this, I heard it . . .'

'Heard what?' said Dan. But of course he knew.

'James's harmonica. The sound coming from the porch of your house – and I thought the tune being played about the most beautiful that had ever fallen on my ears: charged with longing, and yet exciting, exuberant too. I turned my head, and saw your brother, his hands cupped round his mouth, and a look of rapture on his face.'

Yes, thought Dan, yes, *El Ecstático*!

'His hair, all tousled like a much younger person's, seemed the same colour as the cut corn stooked in the fields. I wanted to salute him, to go up to him and tell him how his tune affected me – just like *you* did to *me* last night – but I hadn't the courage. And he didn't appear to have noticed me. And then, just as he had changed from one tune – "Sugar in the Gourd", in point of fact – to another, I heard a voice coming from the hall: "James!" it said, "after a day of intellectual pursuit of the Swan of Avon, I have surely the right to a repast at the time when I desire it! And where *is* it, pray? I can see not even so much as a solitary sign of its preparation. Which cannot be done, may I be so plain-speaking as to remind you, by means of a barbarian musical instrument."'

For an instant, it was as if the grave in the Tanbury cemetery had cracked open, and Pappa, wearing his martyr's cloak, were standing in this forlorn Spanish attic-room.

'Of course when I got back to St. Jude's Vicarage I plied my uncle and aunt with questions about your family, about whom they spoke warmly, if – as I now realise – a trifle guardedly. However, realising my interest, they rang up your father that very night and invited him and James over for drinks on Saturday morning. Perhaps because the week, for all its gentle pleasures, had been so very pastoral and uneventful, so very unlike what I was used to, perhaps because I was still in that febrile state which follows major illnesses, but images of James kept me from sleep for a long time that night. I imagined him playing music just for my delight; I imagined the two of us setting out on adventurous expeditions; I imagined him declaring I was the best friend he had in the world. And in fact two of those came to pass!' Kevin said, blushing and averting his eyes from Dan's, the Biblical expression ringing oddly on his sensual, Cupid's bow lips.

'And then the next morning the strange coincidence occurred.'

The strange coincidence? Dan realised that an important stage in the history had been reached; maybe *that* was why the eyes had been turned away. 'There came a letter from Jason! Wishing me well, hoping I was feeling better, relaying magazine gossip. I was much missed at *Project*, he told me, my stand-in was most unsatisfactory, and so Jason had his hands really full, was not, in fact, having enough time for the writing he did outside the magazine. Naturally I felt a bit guilty about this; Jason had, as I've related, been very kind to me in my illness, and he was not one to complain about his work-load as a rule. But I *could* be of help to him, he went on, yes, even in my Tanbury sojourn. He was going to write an article about one Hampton Varney, and various writers like him, to coincide with the reissue of one of H.V.'s books – *The Sacrament of Grass*. (The very title itself really intrigued me!) It would be a great blessing if I could do the personal research for him; later he'd be sending his mate, Geoffrey Carr, down to get a few details sorted out. But if I could write – or even telephone him – giving him an account of what Hampton Varney's present life was like, it didn't matter whether the details I supplied were trivial, or frivolous – well, I'd more than justify my absence in his eyes. One thing, though! it would be better for me when carrying out my research not to mention the name of Jason Fletcher. It might inhibit communication.'

'Might inhibit!' exclaimed Dan, 'it might indeed have done!' He saw now in his mind's eye this racy, persuasive letter from Jason (and who was better at being both than his former friend?) and then his brother, a few months later in Bencroft, after E.C.T. treatment, thin and white-complexioned, eyes unseeing and body in the grip of a spasm. Perhaps it wasn't going to be as easy to bear with Kevin's narrative as he'd thought.

Kevin, of course, was not unaware of what was passing through his mind. '*Please* hear me out, Dan,' he said, and once again Dan thought how his eyes resembled rain-covered sloes, 'I'm not attempting to justify myself; you can think what you like about me: I'll deserve any contempt you show. But I want you to know *everything* that happened in Tanbury last year, and from *my* point of view. And it's only fair to remember that I had personal debts to Jason, which I did not have to your family, that I didn't really know what was behind all this and maybe still don't know everything, and that I thought the whole "commission", as Jason always called it, not only rather fun, but a Heaven-sent opportunity for getting to know the one person in Tanbury to whom I felt drawn.'

Heaven-sent, thought Dan bitterly.

'Go on,' he said, 'I'll hear you to the end!' And he poured himself out another mug of the dark, curiously gritty tea. So this was how Jason had come by his intimate details of life at 'The Cedars'; the story was now piecing itself together like the severed limbs joining up to form the whole murdered body in that old Greek legend.

'I don't know that there *is* an end,' said Kevin ruefully, 'or do I mean that I hope there isn't? Anyway I'd reached the Saturday when your father and brother came over to the Vicarage for drinks before lunch, hadn't I? I now look back on that day, for all its eventual aftermath, as one of the few really joyful ones in my life.

'I woke up with the conscious recognition that I was physically stronger. By the end of the next week who knew what height of robustness I would have attained? I finished *The Story of a Red Deer* and found myself regretting how little I knew about wild animals; theirs was a world I'd have to look into. Then I did a bit of air-gun practice – with *non-living* targets, of course; my uncle had found the weapon in the cellar, and I found the exercise novel and challenging – I had a good eye, so I was far better at shooting than I would have anticipated. Afterwards I went shopping for my aunt in Tanbury, and I suddenly felt curiously at one with all the people in the market-square – the swarthy-looking stall-holders from the country, the housewives haggling for fruit and vegetables, the young boys and girls examining the *bric-à-brac* and clothes and second-hand L.P.s – never before had I experienced the sense of belonging to a crowd which was fundamentally amiable. After this pleasant morning I walked back to the Vicarage – it was a crisp sunny day, with that autumnal peppermint tang in the air – and I remember thinking: "I am at the beginning of something important in my life!" Well,' and he gave a melancholy giggle, 'I suppose I was!

'Aunt Frances had made the Vicarage drawing-room look very pretty for the visitors – with Michaelmas daisies in all the vases, and old Chinese bowls on the table full of plums and those very small, sweet pears she grows. Uncle Edward saw to the drinks tray; he was, however, a little *distrait* this morning because he'd received a letter from an antiquarian book- and picture-dealer, telling him of a Thomas Bewick engraving depicting a chicken remarkably like one of his own "baggy-trousered" ones.

'And then the doorbell rang, and there were your father and brother. As I heard their voices in the hall, I knew that I was right to have felt so excited, and that my meeting with them was going to be a decisive one. Well,' and he gave another giggle, 'I scored a bull's eye *there*, didn't I?

'James entered my aunt and uncle's maidenly, genteel room – well, you *know* it – like, I thought, some vigorous personification of the harvest. Remember I'd only seen him in the evening shadows on your porch. Even then, as I've said, I'd noticed how his hair was the colour of corn, but not how his blue eyes resembled the flowers you find at the cornfields' edges. He was wearing blue jeans and a red-and-black-checked shirt. He gave me an open, pleased sort of smile, and he shook my hand hard and heartily. He said he hoped I was enjoying myself here. But at that point our interchange was interrupted by your father who had stridden into the room alongside my uncle with regal steps. "Edward," he cried, and turning to my aunt, "and Frances, of course, too – what think you of *this*?" Dan, the room might have been a stage he was about to take possession of. He pulled out of the pocket of his shapeless corduroys a folded piece of paper which turned out to be the proof of the blurb for the new edition of *The Sacrament of Grass*. I'm afraid I know every word.' (So did Dan, but he gave himself the masochistic pleasure of hearing the whole thing again.)

'"It is our belief that the public which has of recent years responded so fervently to the works of the Powys Brothers and of Knut Hamsun will be equally stirred by the writings of the too-little-known Hampton Varney, 'that man of Oxfordshire', as he is proud to call himself. For all his deep-rootedness in a locality, he never looks at the world around him save with a universal eye – 'an elemental eye', to use *his* words, 'a visionary eye', to use *ours*. This novel – in print again after almost forty years – tells of the growth to manhood of the very English Cedric in the Cots-

wold countryside, locked in the struggle between the forces of
Life and the forces of Death."

' "Hampton, what a beautiful tribute!" said my aunt, while
"*Spiffing*, simply spiffing!" spluttered my uncle. Your father, casting
his own very blue eyes about the room as if in search of a vaster
and even more enthusiastic audience, said: "I don't think I could
have written a better description of the book myself. Perhaps a reference to *Goethe* would not have come amiss, but all the same . . ."

' "Let us drink, then, to the book's success," said Uncle Edward,
clattering the tray, "though I know it won't be gracing the bookshops for another two months. I have here some fine Amontillado
– or there is a bottle of delicious sweet Liebfraumilch which I could
open." Dan – as the two men stood together, upon the carpet, in
a patch of the September sunlight, I couldn't help thinking them
rather alike, for all that your father had a full mane of white hair
and my uncle only a shiny bald pate. "Rhineland wines!" said your
father with a musing, lyrical air, "how they take me back to those
walking tours of my earlier, my most creative years." And he began
to sing an apt verse of *Die Lorelei*:

> *Die Luft ist kuhl, und es dunkelt,*
> *Und ruhig fliest der Rhein;*
> *Der Gipfel des Berges funkelt*
> *Im Abendsonnenschein.'*

I was just thinking how best to describe this absurd performance
for Jason (I am sorry, Dan but I'm telling you *all*), when your father
switched from sentimental song to harsh command. "No *alcohol*
for *James*, remember, Edward. He's on the waggon, as they say,
though what that waggon is or signifies no one has ever explained
to me. He picked up some predictably bad habits during his unfortunate stay in Uncle Sam's country." '

'Poor James,' said Dan feelingly, 'what he's had to go through!'

'Poor James was exactly how I felt, and I glanced at him to
see how he'd taken your father's unkind public reminder of his
apparent weakness. I could see no emotion whatever on his healthy,
handsome face. The conversation turned back to *The Sacrament of*

Grass – which we duly toasted – and it was not for some minutes that James and I had an opportunity of talking to each other again. He asked me in a tone both breezy and formal (many Americans combine these two attributes – have you noticed? Did James pick up this tone in the States, or did he have it beforehand?), "This your first time in Tanbury?"

' "Oh, no. I used to come here quite a lot when I was a small boy, but I haven't really stayed here for years. I've come here to get better from an illness," I told him.

' "To get *better!*" said James, as if amazed, though I realise now the same was really true of him, "you mean, to have yourself diverted by all the hectic social life here!"

' "No, hectic social life's just what I've come to escape from," I said, thinking not of dances and dinner parties, but of "The Coleherne" and "The Salisbury" . . .

'James looked at me with quickened interest. I knew then that he must himself have a raunchy past behind him, though I also knew, of course, that it wouldn't have entailed activities such as my own. "You're in search of quiet and serenity, eh?" he said, "well you've made a good choice in Tanbury – at any rate where the *first* is concerned. Really we're all seething within here, you know!" and then his eyes seemed to register me properly; before, they had not. "Hey," he said, "it was *you* I saw gawping at me from the other side of the lane the evening before last, wasn't it? When I was playing my mouth-organ?"

'For some reason I felt not at all shy of James. Normally a bluff manner like his (like his *was*, I suppose I should say) makes me all too aware that I'm . . . that I'm pansy.' (Again the difficulty in bringing out a word so invariably used derisively.) 'But there was something frank and non-judgemental about him that I took to there and then. "I stopped because I liked so much the way you played," I told him. "I'd never heard anything quite like it before."

' "Well, no," said James, "you wouldn't have done. Not unless you're an enthusiast of Bluegrass or Cajun music, and I shouldn't think you are – not *yet!*" And he gave me another smile – this one seeming to banish those elements of formality of our conversation so far. "But it seems to me like you've the makings of an enthusiast. I've been keen on all that stuff for the Lord knows how many years, and then I went to America to learn it more deeply. And there I . . ."

' "James!" your father's voice resounded across the room, "I trust you are not regaling my friends' young visitor with tales of America. I don't think your experiences there would make very – shall we say, *wholesome* hearing for a young man on the threshold of life."

'I had a strong desire to shout across the drawing-room some of my own naughtier adventures at "The Subway" or as a result of loitering after closing-time outside "The Coleherne". For, *this* time, I could see that James *was* snubbed – worse, wounded – and also that in a curious way he took this as his due. I felt very sorry for him. When the conversation started up again among the three senior people in the room, I said in a low voice to him: "You can tell me about America some other time if you like." "Particularly San Francisco," I was about to add, and then thought better of it. "And I'd love to hear you play more of your kind of music."

' "You really would?" James was sincerely pleased, I could tell. "Well," he said, "that shouldn't be too difficult to arrange. I've a fair amount of time on my hands; I'm not exactly on the Managing Board of I.B.M., am I?"

' "What is it that you do do?" I asked.

' "Kevin," said James with a kind of grave grin, " – it *is* Kevin, isn't it? – you ought never to ask anyone that. Wait till he or she tells you first. I *do* a lot of things, oh, a real lot – but as for a job, well, jobs and me just don't agree." I thought of *Project* where – Jason's presence apart – I'd not really been so happy, and wondered whether the same statement wasn't true of me as well. "Instead I look after my father – his house, his affairs etc." He caught me glancing at your father who was standing by the window, his head thrown back like a lion about to roar. "Not a very thankful task, you're thinking. But I think he needs me, and it's something to be needed – especially when you've fucked up as many things as I have. Actually" – his voice descended into a whisper, "actually I've got something planned to coincide with the reissue of his book that will really please him, I think." . . . Oh, *Dan*,' Kevin broke off, 'it makes one's heart ache, doesn't it? And I had no idea . . .'

'No,' said Dan gently, 'how could you have?' A short silence ensued – stern geese walking over exposed, unrestful graves! No traces remained in Dan of his earlier incipient anger with Kevin. Indeed the affectionate light in which he was presenting James was enabling him to see the brother he had once had, and had loved so much, as nothing in recent years had done.

'He didn't say any more about that "something" – either then or at any other time,' Kevin resumed, 'he spoke instead of various improvements he'd made at "The Cedars". "You can come round to my home any time you like," he said, almost abruptly, "I'd be mighty glad to see you, and there are a few jobs you could give me a hand with, if you felt so inclined. For instance I want to lay in a really big store of logs – I've heard that winter's going to start early this year and will go on for a long time."

'Once again your father was pleased to interrupt. "Bestowing invitations, are you, James?" he said, "well, of course, Gavin . . ."

' "Kevin," James corrected.

' "Kevin, then," said your father, implying that it didn't matter what I was called. "*Kevin* can visit our house whenever he chooses. My only fear – Edward, Frances – " he bowed towards my uncle and aunt, "is whether for your nephew, who stands, one might say," he searched for a phrase and then found the one he'd employed only minutes back, "who stands on the very threshold of life, James's company would be at *all* beneficial."

'I – and, I could observe, my uncle and aunt too – were consumed with embarrassment at these words. I found myself rubbing one of the purple plums against my cheek in confusion, causing a sombre stain to spread on it. But your father went on addressing me: "If you don't heed my son when he speaks about wine or women – I use these words inclusively, to suggest a way of life – then yes, hie ye to 'The Cedars' by all means, and right welcome!"

'My uncle said: "I think it would be very nice for Kevin to spend some time with James, if he could be so good as to entertain him. It's a bit dull for the lad shut up with two old fogeys like my sister and myself. And Kevin, if you've a mind to, you can learn much from James about gardening; what he's done to the garden in 'The Cedars' in so short a time is little short of miraculous. And I'm someone who's *professionally* concerned with miracles." He chuckled. James looked up at him with blue eyes shining with gratitude. "Of course," Uncle Edward continued reflectively, "you could say that in *my* garden flora has been sacrificed to fauna. To the dear Baggy Trousered Chickens. No good for the pot, I'm afraid, and their eggs are nothing to write home about, but when it comes to intelligence," and his voice deepened, "as I always say, there isn't a chicken their equal!" After that it was only natural that the conversation should move on to the Bewick engraving which featured this remarkable bird . . .'

'I went round to "The Cedars" that very afternoon. And after that, for the next fortnight, scarcely a day passed without my visiting your house. (Also James – though less frequently – would call round at the Vicarage.) I did indeed help to chop up and stack wood for your winter store; I picked apples and nuts, and assisted in the repairs to the back garden wall and in the repainting of the scullery and the downstairs cloakroom and lavatory. We worked, for the greater part, in a relaxed, companionable silence, something for me both novel and refreshing. James rarely asked me about myself, and when he did it was never to probe, only to inquire whether I liked or disliked such-and-such a thing. And I returned the compliment, for that's what I felt it to be, and stifled the very considerable curiosity I felt about his obviously troubled past. He said he'd had a tough time of it in the States, though he added that nothing could diminish his love for its music. It was, after all, he said, music intended for tough times.

'When we'd done as much of a particular task as we felt that day required, then James would take out one of his musical instruments – by his preference and mine, the harmonica, and play to me – "Raggerty Annie", "Johnny's Down the River!", "Cotton-blossom Special", "Arkansas Traveller", "Log Cabin," "Down Yonder" – I'll know every note of those tunes as long as I live. As a small boy, like so many others, I'd tried my mouth on the harmonica, but with no great success. Now, intoxicated by your brother's playing, I became an apt pupil, and James showed me various techniques used by musicians in the American South – to produce their particular haunting, passionate sounds – techniques which, by myself, I perfected later on, when my friendship with James had come to its involuntary end.

'Absorbed in both the jobs and the music that he chose for me, never feeling that I had to be seductive or amusing on the one hand, or conventionally manly and self-denyingly sensible on the other, I knew, those two weeks, an intense but peaceful and non-obsessive happiness which grew with each day, and I knew too a love for James as I had never felt for anyone else before. While I wanted, with every drop of my heart's blood, for our time together to continue for ever, I knew that it wouldn't, and not only because I had to go back to London and *Project*. Because I . . . because I *loved* him, I saw that James's life in Tanbury was at best only a half-life, that he was living in a state of reluctant hiding from a world by which he'd been hurt in so many ways, and that there would come a time when he would be able to support this retreat no more. But so content was I that these sad thoughts didn't trouble me as much as you would think; perhaps through the steadiness of my companionship I could prepare James for going back to a fuller existence?'

'Kevin!' said Dan. Oh, how he wanted to embrace him – not from desire, but from gratitude at the goodness of these words.

'The annual fair came to Tanbury the following weekend, and on the Saturday evening James and I went to it. The old buildings of the square seemed quite dwarfed by all the gaudy paraphernalia. When I saw how adept James was with a quoit – and even more so with a rifle – how dashingly he drove a Dodgem car, how daring he became when confronted with the Wall-of-Death and the more giddying wheels and switchbacks, and how he loved the blaring hurdy-gurdy music and the rough badinage of the crowd – and when I contrasted all this with his solitary, almost hermit-like days and your father speaking so contemptuously to him, then I felt a surge of terrible pity for him. But he wasn't feeling any such pity for himself; he appeared to be enjoying himself with all his boy-like body and being.

'The night before I was due to leave Tanbury he said that he wanted to take me to Foxton Woods. To see if we could catch a glimpse of badgers, making from a sett he knew for the stream. After daylight had ended, we set out from "The Cedars" on bikes, and I remember that as we rode down the narrow lanes towards the distant Cotswolds over which the sun was setting, he spoke of *you*, Dan, and with such admiration and affection. Going to Foxton

Woods had been something you'd both loved to do together in your boyhood, he told me. I recall trying to imagine what you'd be like – never imagining that just over a year later, in a foreign country, I'd end up in the same bed as you. You sounded intellectual, serious, kind . . . as you are, I presume?' And for the first time that night that teasing expression appeared on Kevin's face, though not for long. But it was abruptly succeeded by another. 'Actually, James spoke mostly about your knowledge of badgers. He told me some extraordinary fact about important old badgers being accorded ceremonial burials by other badgers, with rabbits and even moles employed as grave-diggers.'

Dan wondered why Kevin's tone was so anxious a one. The piece of folklore could hardly have touched him very nearly. 'It's not fact,' he said, 'at least it may be, but it's not one that's been established. It's a piece of North Country folklore actually, but I've always liked to believe it. Better naturalists than I have. I remember telling James about it on the night of my seventeenth birthday.'

'I half-expected to see the ritual that evening,' said Kevin, 'but we didn't, of course – didn't, in fact, even see any badgers at all. I didn't mind too much, however, for what was better than sitting there beside James in the heart of the wood – listening to the birds calling to each other and to the mysterious passages of unseen creatures through the undergrowth? I felt such pride in him, and such a feeling of safety – even though I knew I was going to be separated from him in twenty-four hours' time. There was one strange thing, though.'

'What was that?' asked Dan.

'James said – suddenly, he must have been thinking again of your legend: "There could be many worse fates, couldn't there? than to be buried in these woods by badgers and rabbits." I agreed with him. The wood had produced a solemnity in me, and the words didn't seem as disturbing as they did later.

'Anyway, James then took out the harmonica he'd been concealing in his jacket pocket, and began to play on it – with particular inventiveness. Then he handed the instrument to me, and I played upon it too – less inventively, but not badly for a beginner. And from then on, for half an hour, back and forth the mouth-organ went. Like the Pipe of Peace among Red Indians.'

It was a joyous, moving image, but Dan felt he could not allow it to be too long lingered upon. 'And the *letters* you were asked to write about life at "The Cedars", the espionage work?' he said, 'I take it you *did* comply with Jason's request. Otherwise certain things wouldn't have appeared in *The Observer* colour supplement article, and otherwise there'd be no need for this guilt and self-recrimination.'

Kevin looked away from Dan now, stared down at the tatty rug upon the floor. 'Yes, I wrote Jason letters,' he said, 'and I must tell you that a good portion of them were taken up with lavish eulogies to James. But I made a good many tart comments about your father's self-centred way of life and his treatment of your brother. Because that was what interested me most. I know one shouldn't speak ill of the dead and all that, and that he *was* your father, but nonetheless . . .'

'You knew the point behind Jason's article, I take it?' said Dan. 'You haven't referred to that yet.'

Kevin's face attempted a look of blankness, but there was such unmistakable dread in his eyes that this piece of mime was wasted. Nevertheless, 'Point?' he repeated, perhaps to give himself time.

'Come on, you're not stupid,' said Dan, 'my father was a Mosleyite, a Fascist. Jason wanted to attack the resurrection of writers like him who had such sympathies, and that's fair enough! Didn't he make you party to that intention? Didn't you know that you were spying to help him with his hatchet-job?'

'No!' said Kevin, and the quick, almost relieved way in which he spoke told Dan that this was the truth.

'But while you were at Tanbury you realised?'

Kevin made no answer. His lower lip was trembling again – as it had at the beginning of their conversation.

'I'm so afraid you won't believe me, Dan,' he said, 'I wouldn't if I were in your place. But I had *no* idea whatever. I'm not a political animal, you see, and not very well up in literary history either. When I read Jason's article, that Sunday, that was the first I knew of it. Things fell into place then, of course.

'But when I got back from Tanbury to London – to the *Project* office which seemed now, after my friendship with James, an unreal, hurrying, superficial place of work, Jason did drop me

hints which I should have picked up, had I been brighter. But like
I told you last night, I've a mind like a butterfly, and I'm afraid I
didn't.

'But his remarks made me uneasy enough to worry about the
article to which I'd, I'd sort of *contributed*. Worried enough to
invite myself back to St. Jude's Vicarage the weekend it was due
to appear. It was James's birthday on the Saturday; he said that
he'd spend the day itself with your father, but that on Sunday he'd
organise a celebration of some kind.

'On the Saturday night I could hardly sleep. On Sunday morning
I asked to be let off attending my uncle's service, saying I was
very tired. I just waited, tense – like I imagine a fox does, when
it is expecting the hounds and huntsmen – for the arrival of *The
Observer*.

'. . . As a matter of fact, and I suppose it's tactless of me to say it
now, but it wasn't as bad as I feared. It quoted remarks your father
had made before the War and which certainly hadn't been supplied
by me: all about how Oswald Mosley was surely clad in the robe
of a hero, that the first duty of an Englishman was to preserve the
purity of English blood, that usury and those who served it deserved
no habitation in a civilised but Nature-honouring land . . .'

'You've no need to quote,' said Dan, 'I remember them. But
– the picture of Pappa writing at a desk dominated by busts of
Shakespeare and Goethe, his "pilgrimages" – as he liked to call
them – to Stratford to feel in time with the spirit of his Great
Mentor, his being waited on by a son he tyrannised – Jason didn't
make a very flattering portrait emerge from those details, and they
were based on *your* material, I think.'

'I suppose,' muttered Kevin.

'Come off it,' said Dan, 'no supposing about it. You know they
were!'

'Let me go on,' said Kevin, and suddenly Dan realised that
the telling of the tale was costing him a great deal physically and
emotionally. Looking at him now it was not hard to believe that
only a year ago he'd been seriously, perhaps dangerously ill. 'I went
round to "The Cedars". The car was in the drive, the door was
open. I rang the bell, but could make no one hear. I then became
aware of raised voices in the kitchen.'

Dan thought what an odd parallel this made to his own visit to St. Jude's Vicarage that time when – mistakenly, he often now thought – he'd asked Father Lalland about the wisdom of James's emigrating to America. But Kevin was going to describe no such innocent emergence from a house as that of an errant Baggy Trousered Chicken. Kevin was continuing: 'I shouted out, "Hullo, anyone there? It's me, Kevin."' Dan could not but be a little melted by the childlike tone Kevin reproduced as he repeated his call into the hall of 'The Cedars'; perhaps after all he really *had* been the innocent abroad in the whole grim territory of the matter, which he'd presented himself as being. 'Still no answer. So I took the liberty of entering the house uninvited. Your father and brother were opposing one another across the kitchen table, the Sunday paper spread out between them. "But you told me yourself that *you* personally arranged for the article to be published," your father was shouting, "you damned traitor! You serpent's tooth! How well I understand the old Jewish saying about the ungrateful son! To have contrived to have your father made a mock of, his philosophy – which unites the two noblest strands of the West – and his perforce reduced lifestyle treated as a joke. And his relations with his son – a son who had to be rescued from drunkenness, whoring and debts – dragged out as a matter for hostile public criticism . . . *James*, henceforth how can I regard you as a son?"'

How often had Dan imagined this scene, and its immediate predecessor – James boasting proudly to Pappa that he'd got him an article all to himself in *The Observer*, his carrying the newspaper in triumph into the kitchen, the two of them bending over the opened supplement, Pappa's initial exclamation of joy . . . But Kevin was continuing:

'That's another thing I hadn't realised, you see, Dan. That James had *asked* Jason to write the article.'

'I didn't imagine Jason *would* have told you *that*,' said Dan wryly. But – during those early visits to Bencroft – the fact had been burned into Dan's brain by its tearful reiteration by James. And as he'd listened to his brother, Dan had always seen before him Jason Fletcher's clever, grinning, catlike face. And had heard him laugh in that light, sarcastic manner that had distinguished him as a sixth-former. And had longed to see him – as in real life he never had – the victim of James's fists in the Grammar School pavilion.

'You must tell me what happened next?' he made himself ask.

'At first I thought James wasn't going to defend himself,' said Kevin, 'the silence – it was like a wave crashing down upon rocks and drenching everything. But at last your brother *did* speak:

' "All right, Pappa," he said, "believe what you bloody want to of me!" His eyes were different from how I'd ever seen them before. They were now a fierce, *cruel* blue. "After all it'd figure, wouldn't it? You've never thought well of me, never! I've tried to please you, tried to serve you, tried to be a good son to you – God help me, if I haven't. So now you can fucking think what you want about me!"

'And then he lunged forward. Dan, his fist haunts me even now. It seemed so horribly huge and luminous as it came forward towards your father's face.'

'So he did actually attack Pappa,' said Dan. He had never been quite sure of this; he had been hoping, he now realised, that Kevin would prove it not to have been the case.

'Your father dodged the blow,' said Kevin, 'James's fist met the wall – the impact must have been extremely painful for him. But he prepared himself for another attack. And then . . . and then he caught sight of *me* in the doorway.' His voice cracked on this last sentence.

'So what did you do?' Dan asked. Never had he imagined a third person present at this so intimate battle.

'Dan,' said Kevin softly, 'you don't need to know any more. Truly you don't! After all, weren't you there yourself at "The Cedars" the next day? Your father and Dr. Cardew called you, didn't they? . . . "My elder son!" "My brother!" – *that's* how I heard you spoken of,' he added with a sad attempt at a winsome smile, 'they never called you Dan. Certainly not like *I* have.'

Their intimacy was something that Dan would prefer at this moment not to dwell on. 'Did you ever see James again?' he asked, realising he was going to get no more exact account of the scene in the kitchen.

'Not after that day,' said Kevin. His words were barely audible.

Then followed a silence such as Kevin had recently described breaking over 'The Cedars'. Dan himself was by now too tired,

too confused to find a sentence with which to end it. But Kevin
was able eventually to ask pleadingly: 'Do you hate me very much,
Dan? There must be a part of you that wants to kill me.'

Of course Dan told him there was not. He then made himself
stay there in the ghastly attic and ask Kevin questions about his
interests and his Madrid life, questions that would prove to him
that no bitterness, no anger prevailed. Kevin could not have been
much fooled. For one thing Dan could hardly bring himself to look
at the boy, and addressed many of his remarks to the covered bird-
cage.

Nor was he much taken with the picture of Kevin that emerged
from their stilted conversation. His taste in art struck him as so
much camp self-indulgence, his free life in the streets and bars a
sort of blasphemy against love and liberty – a blasphemy, he added
to himself grimly, in which he had colluded.

Finally he got up. How late it must be! But he ought to leave
this unfortunate – not night-*hawk* but -*dove* – on a kindly, forgiving
note, whatever the cost to himself. He made himself pat Kevin on
the back (that which he had kissed so amorously last night) and
say: 'You must realise, Kevin, that I understand what guts it's taken
for you to tell me what you have this evening. And the situation
was not . . . not of your making.'

He felt Kevin turn moist, grateful eyes upon his face, and, to his
astonishment and dismay, a current of sexual desire assailed him.

His mouth emptied of saliva, as so often in moments of
apprehension combined with lust. Something made him go on:
'If, Kevin, by any chance you want to come to the lecture at the
University tomorrow, I'd be pleased to see you in the audience.
Richard – Dr. Cardew of Tanbury's son will be there too. There'll
be refreshments. You could stay for those and meet some of my
colleagues.' That'll be fun for him, he thought, and certainly interesting for them! Why, he'll be the subject of gossip for them all
until next year's conference!

There could be no escaping the intensity of Kevin's look now.
Nor of his stance: 'I'd certainly like to hear your lecture, a lot,' he
said, 'but . . . but what I'd like most,' and his words tumbled out
in a fervent rush, 'is to come back with you to England. Dan, I felt
that so strongly last night. Because what we made together was

so beautiful. Didn't you think so? And when I realised what lay between us, all the terrible secrets, it broke my heart. Which had gone out to you in *love*, Dan! But now there are no secrets between us. And my heart is still in the same condition. Let me return with you to England as your *amante* as they say here in Spain (so much better a word than "boyfriend" or even "lover"). I'll look after you, I'll be warm and good to you; Daniel Varney need never be lonely again when Kevin Lalland's with him. He'll care for him with every inch of his being and with all his might.'

Arms were tightly wound around him, and a wet, bony, beautiful face was pressed against his. All the need for and tenderness towards the boy experienced last night swept over Dan anew, and with surely greater force.

'I can't pay for my whole fare back right now,' said Kevin, speaking into Dan's breast, 'but I *can* give you *something* towards it, and the rest I'll make up later, I promise. I'll have to – in order to show my sincerity, won't I?' He withdrew from Dan and said: 'I don't hear any words of fervent pleasure, do I? Daft of me to expect them, I suppose. If you can bear it, I'm going to wind my history up for you. You can stay a little longer. What I say might make you melt towards me a little.

'After what had happened, I *couldn't* work for Jason and *Project* any more, and getting a new job was almost impossible. You know how it is in journalism and publishing in England now. And my parents weren't very sympathetic to me. The question of my sexual preference was now brought up for the severe discussion it hadn't received when I'd confessed it – no job, and a little queen in the making, I was properly beyond the pale I was.

'So I decided that I'd up and leave. Where? The day of my decision I met and slept with an American of about your age, who told me that for gay life Madrid was one of Europe's best capitals. They even advertise the fact in the official guide – and that's only six years after Franco! When I got home the next morning, I saw open in the drawing-room one of my father's books on *Los Reyes Católicos*. So Spain and Madrid it had to be! And I must say I haven't regretted it.

'But it's been often extremely lonely, and there are times, you know, when, even for someone like me, "trading" isn't exactly the most soul-satisfying of occupation. But one day a good man will come along, I've always said to myself. And then last night you came. And by the strangest coincidence in the world you were connected with the two people who have shaped my present life. Through you I can make it up with Jason – for I'd like to, you know – and through you I can help your brother. Why,' and his face lit up, 'you and I could give him back his *Hohner* harmonica *together*.' And he smiled as if in inner contemplation of this beatific scene.

'But I don't want you to think that it isn't for yourself that I care for you. Because it is; it *is*!'

The embrace was resumed, more tightly. Lips were upon his lips, cock was hard against his own crutch . . . Perhaps after all Dan *had* known it would all end this way. To have this loving, complex, wounded boy with him – for always, maybe – would be a gift so wonderful that no thanks to any heaven would be enough. This didn't mean that there wouldn't be many difficulties ahead of them, but their mutual need, their shared gentleness, their shared resolutions would surely carry them through.

Dan remembered his thoughts in the Rastro at lunchtime. Impairedness and wholeness . . . To live with a vision of the whole, that was essential. But to expect it in others, that was a cruel mistake. Rather one must see in another Wholeness' shattered reflection, and often it was in precisely the more intolerable idiosyncrasies that his or her nearest approximation to the dazzling sun of Virtue could be found. Kevin's oscillations and weaknesses, his tendency towards duplicity, his desire for approbation, his sexual vanity and appetite – here, as well as in his obvious sensitivity, his soul and its aspirations after the Good, the Beautiful, the True, received, he had little doubt, an expression which one must not only accept but honour.

'We leave for England tomorrow then,' he said, 'together!' Dan pressed his tongue hard into Kevin's mouth. And then – James in Nashville! he thought. He must see that *this* loved one he was bringing back to his homeland had a happier time there.

It was, however, not of Kevin or James, but of Pappa that Dan found himself thinking as he walked back through the quiet old streets of Chueca to his hotel. Why had Hampton Varney never believed in his second son's innocence? Why had he never seen the need for his love and admiration that had consumed James? How often in the six months between the departure for Bencroft and Pappa's sudden death from a heart-attack had Dan urged his father to visit James, to ring him up, write to him. To no avail! *'You're* the only son I have, Dan,' Pappa would reply, 'I have no energy these days to be vexed by one that has renounced son-hood through reviling his father.' 'But . . .' Dan would begin, knowing that James had written to Jason and *The Observer* for no other purpose but to bring Pappa belated glory – but the old man was deaf to fact and reason.

In those six months, though, while James lived away from the world, Pappa and he had enjoyed a satisfying *second* relationship. No longer father and son, merely two men who found in dealing with one another a curiously healing and tender solicitude. The trouble with Pappa had been, Dan had thought – realising, however, that this could only be a partial explanation – that he had not been humanly engaged enough to comprehend the forces he'd chosen to salute. There was no need to ask what Pappa would have thought of the Franquistas of today's demonstrations: he would have disliked them very much. Had he ever been able to bring his brain to bear upon the individual case, he would indeed have found the Caudillo, Franco's behaviour, government and morals abhorrent. But he couldn't so concentrate, had let self-centred dreams carry him beyond the point where examination of what was happening to real human beings was important. And that anti-human streak had also enabled him to consign poor James to a cruel oblivion. Dan had been a good son, James an unsatisfactory one, and that had sufficed.

How wonderful then that Dan had come to Madrid and that the boy he had chosen to pick up in the Recoletos had been Kevin Lalland. Together they could release James from that oblivion!

The eaves of the venerable, dignified houses in this street cast huge shadows upon the narrow pavement. In one of these shadows a young man was standing, his face generously covered in dark stubble, a pile of hand-outs tucked underneath his arm.

'*Buenas noches!*' he called out to Dan from his patch of darkness.

'*Buenas noches!*' Dan felt obliged to reply.

'*Inglés?*'

'Yes!'

The boy came out of the shadow, 'Some of these papers of mine here are in English,' he said in Dan's language, speaking in a stilted way, as a marionette might, 'and I would much like to give you one!' He began to fumble through the hand-outs.

'I'm afraid,' Dan made himself say, 'that I'm no sympathiser with the Franquista cause. It's only honest to tell you.'

'But – *no me!*' said the boy indignantly, 'I am anti-Fascist, like all my family for two generations.'

'I'm sorry,' Dan mumbled. And indeed, seeing the injured expression on the boy's face, he truly was.

'It's an easy mistake for a foreigner to make on a day of demonstrations,' the boy replied, 'but look at this paper, please,' (this was difficult to do; the moonlight upon the street was not quite bright enough, and there was no street-lamp near-by) 'here you can read the translation my friend Joaquín and I have made of a poem of freedom by José-Miguel Yuste Martínez. It says that the day will soon come when those who want the military way, the way of blackness, will be as unreal as night is when it is day-light. Underneath the brilliant sun of Andalucía – *I* am from Andalucía,' he added, in a proud parenthesis, 'and so is José-Miguel, from *Red Andalusia* – Spanish democracy will flourish and spread. Socialists will be as olives in an orchard, as tuna-fishes in the seas off Cadiz, as upright sunflowers in the fields of the Andalusian *labradores* . . . Oh, in Spanish it sounds very beautiful. But in English?' He gesticulated sadly, realising that Joaquín and he hadn't made as good a job of the translation as they'd hoped.

'In English it sounds beautiful too,' Dan told him, 'and I'll be proud to keep a copy of this poem.'

The encounter somehow set a noble seal on the fraught day, with its night of confessions and promises and straining hopes.

'Come back to Spain in a year's time,' the boy said, giving Dan the hand-out with an oddly grand gesture, a street courtier's, 'and you will hardly be able to believe that this day was true!'

It wasn't until long afterwards that Dan said to himself: All days are true!

When James woke up two or three hours after he'd gone to bed, he didn't, for a few moments, know where he was. Walls were not in the right places, they were pressing upon him from unanticipated angles. And where was the light? where the window? He couldn't be in his *coffin* already, could he? He began to grope, to pat alien surfaces. Just before he permitted himself a scream, his hand encountered what could be the base of a lamp. Apprehensively he worked it upwards until it found a switch, which he pressed. Thank *God*! He was not in his coffin nor in his old bleak, aseptic room in Bencroft. He was in the 'boy's' room at St. Jude's Vicarage, the boy being Kevin Lalland. Before him stretched the cheerful, somehow virginal patchwork quilt which covered the bed; on the floor lay a red Turkish carpet patterned in green and old gold; at the window (which was not, after all, hard to find) hung chintz curtains; there was a bookcase crammed with florid-spined Victorian and Edwardian children's books, and on the walls hung old engravings of wild animals – fox, hare, stoat, mole, and yes – best of all – his and Dan's favourite, badger.

Last year Kevin had slept here, Kevin who was now for some odd reason in Spain, Kevin who apparently had looked up to *him*, James, more than he'd done to anyone else, and to whom he had been very kind. James tried to fasten his mind on the months of September and October last year, when this relationship must have flourished. He made himself see the golden light so peculiar to that time of year, the apples and nuts in the orchards, the cornstooks in the fields, the trees on the turn, the mist that rises from streams in the evenings and fills woods. And suddenly, like a visitation, Kevin came back to him. How could he have been absent so long? With perfect clarity James saw now the boy's thin, freckled, dark-eyed face and the quizzical way he'd look at you as if pleading for approval, for liking. And the surprised satisfaction that had spread over his whole being when he'd mastered a tune

on the harmonica in the manner that James had demonstrated to
him.

Yes, he *had* been kind to Kevin Lalland. For he had liked him,
had sensed in him a vulnerability, a waywardness, a deep innocence and a craving for affection, no, for *love*, that reminded him
of himself. And yet Kevin had been 'other' as well: soft, sensuous,
unashamedly, yes, so unashamedly tender. Oh, yes, now he'd recovered him, he knew that he wanted – ardently – to see the lad
again. He'd like to play to him again, to take him once more to
Tanbury Fair, and into Foxton Woods to wait for badgers. Indeed
he might there tell Kevin about – or even (who knew?) introduce
him to – that secret which had consoled him with its mystery and
beauty, in all this long year of imprisonment and despair.

James glanced at the bedside clock: only one-thirty. He would
try to read a little, and then, if he found the right book he could
return to sleep knowing the first earnest of happiness he had experienced for a year. He got out of bed, scanned the shelves, and – his
hand lit upon – of all things! – that recent reprint of Pappa's *Sacrament of Grass*. How detestable had become to him its laminated
jacket bright with a reproduction of one of Paul Nash's most conscientiously green and 'mystical' paintings!

As nervously as if he were handling a parcel that might well
contain a bomb, James made himself open the fatal book. As he
did so, a note fell out of it, dropped on to the Turkish carpet. He
picked it up, and read it – no hard task, for it was very, very brief.
'Dear Kevin,' it said,

'Find enclosed for your Varney research,

Love, Jason.'

So, thought Kevin, as he undressed for bed, Madrid is now jour-
neying towards history for me. And its doing so will bring pain,
however pleased I am to be leaving with Dan. For he would miss
the city, and not just its so ample gay life. He would regret, for
instance, the noisy, almost jolly Metro, the doors of its trains hissing
like amiable snakes as they opened and shut, and the stations that
he had passed through so many times on his way from his rooms
to lovers' apartments, Luis's above all: Chueca, Alonso Martínez,
Rubén Darío (the name of a poet he'd never yet read and perhaps

now never would), Nuñez de Balboa and Diego de Leon, with its long-passaged exit into the ugly but likeable (because so lively) Calle de Francisco Silvela. Somewhere in his mind he would always be travelling through these stations . . .

In winter months Kevin had liked to breakfast on strong coffee and *churros* – those batter-sticks resembling inches of warm, edible copper. In summer all the cafés and bars offered you bowls of cold, piquant Gazpacho soup and carafes of Sangria, with ice and chopped fruit – gastronomic challenges to the too strong and insistent sun.

Sometimes Kevin would walk behind the Royal Palace or the Calle Mayor and see how the great city came to an abrupt stop on crowned cliffs, or go to the gardens beyond the university where many an amorous older gay went strolling. From these points he could see over the rolling grassy country towards the great mountains of the Gredos. Even at hot times of the year these august shapes could be anointed with snow, and – after the confusions of an unoccupied afternoon or before the murky businesses of the night – it was good to raise your eyes to them. And if you feasted long enough on all this loftiness and cold, then you could turn back, eased, to clammy humanity, to the loud, vivacious talk and *Mahous* and *tapas* of the thousand bars of Old Madrid.

All the same he had to leave!

But with Dan? Was that really such a good idea? What about those things he had *not* been able to tell him? They wouldn't remain hidden inside him for ever. How could they?

How hard he had tried to forget what James had said to him that terrible day, as he'd caught sight of him, fearful in the doorway of 'The Cedars' kitchen! But never could he. The words came to him now from across the chasm of a year: 'What the hell are *you* doing here, you fucking little pouff? Take that sissy's ass of yours out of here!'

They had been words from Kevin's most constant, most dreaded nightmare. And on hearing them actually spoken, he'd behaved like a child – had turned away and run out of the house, out of its garden, and down the hill into the town. But they had sounded in his ears, cacophonously, all the rest of the morning, all the afternoon, more persistent and obtrusive than any Sunday church-bell.

Then in the early evening the telephone had rung in the Vicarage drawing-room.

'Kevin,' Uncle Edward had said, in a surprised tone, 'it's Hampton Varney for you.'

The voice on the other end of the line had been almost unrecognisable in its urgency and trouble. 'I'm ringing you because of James,' it said, 'I was hoping you could help me, Kevin. You see he's left me this note. Which I don't understand. But perhaps it'd mean something to *you* . . .'

The note had simply said: 'Pappa, I've gone to the one place where I feel happy and safe. I intend to stay there. James.'

'Do you think he's . . .' But Hampton Varney had been unable to complete the sentence.

How was it that Kevin had known what that 'one place' signified? Perhaps Dan – had he been there – also would have known. In one part of his being, Kevin now felt, he would always be making that nervous journey in the hired car to Foxton, wrapped, in its hollow, in miasmic grey; would always be stumbling through the woods, scratched by briars and wayward branches, with mud and stones and exposed roots hostile underfoot. Stumbling towards the spot where, not so long ago, James and himself had sat, as friends, passing the harmonica back and forth, as though it had been the Pipe of Peace.

James had been there where Kevin had led them all – Uncle Edward, Hampton Varney, the policeman – upon the mossy bank above the stream, beside the badgers' sett. Had stripped himself of clothes, was naked as any other animal of the wood, but shivering, down on all fours and grunting. How he had flailed them with feet and fists when apprehended! How he had snarled, how he had spat! And when finally they'd cornered and captured him, his feral eyes had seemed to be seeing not familiar faces but the countenance of Nothing itself.

At Hampton Varney's request, Kevin had stayed with James all night – in the drawing-room of 'The Cedars'. Dr. Cardew had given him sedatives, James's brother had been contacted and had said he would be in Tanbury by the afternoon. Some time during the day ahead James would be taken away from home – and into 'a Home'. Meanwhile Kevin, devoid of even the temptation to go to sleep, had watched, hour after heavy, quiet hour, over his friend's handsome, unconscious, exhausted form. He'd tried not to think of his own possible responsibility for the day's horrible events; he'd tried not to recall the hateful words James Varney had – at last – spoken to him. But he could not succeed in his stiflings, and every time he'd remembered them – contemptibly into his pity had come stabs of spiteful relish.

Towards dawn James had woken up. 'Still here, old Kevin?' he'd said, in something like his old voice, but with no surprise evident in it, 'you shouldn't be! Not for a bum like me. What's the point? Are you frightened I'll run away again?'

'Perhaps.'

'Well, there's no need. James Varney's got no strength left. Specially after old Cardew's pills. I don't think I could so much as get up from the sofa.'

'You seem a little better,' Kevin had observed, longing to stroke his face, his hair.

'But I'm not feeling it, boyo, you take it from me! My head's nobody's business – but then it never *was* too good. I *knew* what I was doing out there in the woods, you know.' A pause, then: 'Don't look like that at me, Kevin. You've not got to believe it if you don't want to.'

Kevin had let his gaze wander away from James towards the window, the curtains of which were not completely drawn: over the black swellings of the Cotswolds the green light of a new day was pushing itself.

'Kevin, promise me one thing! When you talk to my father in the morning, make him swear that my brother mustn't know what I was up to in the woods. No one must tell him. Foxton Woods were a very special place for the two of us. They'd be ruined for him, if he ever found out about tonight.

'I reckon they're going to shut me up, don't you? *I'd* shut myself up if I were they. So, be a sport and go to that cabinet over there. Bring me my harmonica box which is on top of it. Thanks. *Now,*' placing this in Kevin's hands, 'if you want to do one thing for me, accept this as a present from me. And *play* the damned instrument – as I've said before, you've got all the makings of a first-class player. No, don't hesitate. I really want you to have it, kiddo, and you mustn't be so cruel as to refuse it. After all I don't think I'll be needing it in the place I'm going to.'

And even as he handed the precious object to Kevin, his eyes seemed to be looking upon Nothing again.

Kevin's eyes now filled with tears once more. Tears for himself as well as for James. No, he could not really feel anything but frightened at the prospect of returning to England, James Varney's country, Jason Fletcher's country, and in the company of the brother of the one, the estranged former friend of the other.

Besides, hadn't his life as a seasoned *maricón* made a shared life of constancy an impossibility for him?

Kevin looked at the clock; it wasn't as late as he'd thought. He wondered whether to return to the *Viznaga*.

Death was everywhere he turned. Up in Foxton Woods the badgers lay wounded, bleeding upon the earth in the kindnesses of which they'd made their homes. Kevin's eyes had killed them – as mockingly he recorded James's delight in the creatures. Through the wood the stream carried the trash of pill-bottles – all the sedatives that had imprisoned him in hygienic rooms while his feet yearned for dusty roads and rough company. Valium, librium, barbiturates littered the mossy banks, and no one was sorry. Bright and Thompson executives strode upon them and laughed; Cynthia smashed plates upon them to add to the litter in glee. Jason Fletcher, in a swank suit, his cat's eyes very bright, declared; 'All this is mine now!'

Only Dan was missing from these scenes of despoliation and destruction – Dan who'd always been kind to him, Dan who'd enabled him to go to America to seek his fortune, and had also enabled him to return home. But he'd lost Dan now.

But home – well, that did, in one sense only, remain. In 'The Cedars' the spirit of the past, of what he had formerly for so long desired and thought possible, would be living yet. James turned over in bed, and, for the second time that night, switched on the table-lamp. He would get up, dress, walk over to 'The Cedars' and keep a vigil over the house till morning. Who had been more vigilant, more attentive to it than he? He would take with him Father Lalland's airgun, with which he'd taught Kevin to perfect his aim.

He hardly cared to whom the house now belonged. It seemed a matter of only the very slightest consequence.

Dan sat down at the desk in his hotel room to compose a new conclusion for his lecture. But as his pencil worked, he was travelling, yet again, back to that night of his seventeenth birthday, when James and he had been in Foxton Woods and he had told James of the old legend of badgers receiving solemn funeral-rites, and James had played 'Wildwood Flower' on the harmonica to him.

'You've never played better than that, Jamesie!'

'Well, it can be my birthday present to you, Dan. Only I'll want something in return.'

'It's rather unusual to give conditions for birthday presents!'

'I'm a rather unusual guy!'

'Well, what *is* this condition?'

But Dan had known it. This did not make it any the easier to agree to. He'd looked up into the dark worlds of the trees and wished he could escape to them as one of their denizens, beyond all the tangle of pasts and quarrels and emotional demands.

'You've got to stop going around with that ace shit, Jason Fletcher.'

'That's a pretty steep request, Jamesie!'

'And hasn't that pillock's behaviour also been bloody steep? He *insulted* us this afternoon, Dan. And anyway, haven't you a loyalty to me? After my fight with him, wouldn't it look a bit strange if you continued to be matey-matey with my enemy. As if you didn't put *me* above him.'

In the end, of course, Dan had given his brother a hedged promise. And so had hurt Jason. Thus he too – through weakness, through kindness – had helped to forge the chain that had led to the anguishes of last year and to the strange encounters of the past two days . . .

Concentrate! Concentrate on the demands of the particular! In this instance, his learned paper.

The window of his hotel room gave on to an immense well, in the bare walls of which lights were still burning behind windows. He re-read the whole lecture now – the ending still wasn't right. And yet out of gratitude to what had happened to him in Madrid, he wanted to make his paper at its university his best yet. But . . . again he was seeing the young Franquistas unfurling their aggressive flags, and the kind old hotel porter beseeching him to focus on those aspects of Madrid that were all that the demonstrators were not. He was seeing Goya's saint and his misshapen, painfully risen victim with the speaking wounds; he was seeing *El Ecstático* standing, head tilted back, against jagged rocks. He was seeing the melancholy junk piled on the stalls of the Rastro; he saw Richard bemusedly contemplating the broken plate he'd lovingly bought for his wife. And he was seeing James as he'd been in Nashville, drunk, wretched; he was seeing Kevin as he'd been in the gay club, headband aglow, amid sorry, pleasure-seeking mates, and afterwards in his flat, during the hour of painful revelation and confession, vulnerable, lovable.

Then his head cleared. He could write that different conclusion. Each sentence seemed, as excitedly he penned it, to resemble one of the lighted windows in the hotel well.

'We must do all we can, of course,' his hand declared, 'to alleviate, indeed to remove, the so often desperate miseries which have resulted from not being able to speak as others do. To achieve these alleviations and removals demands knowledgeable recourse to clinical medicine, to practical psychiatry, to the findings of linguistics experts. But we who work in this field must never fall into the all-too-common humanist error of wanting to make a complex, troubled, perhaps troublesome human being outwardly more acceptable and therefore less threatening to us. Let us be mindful of the fact that the person stumbling over words in a painful, and often infuriating, way may be being faithful to some profound relation of inner self to external world which it would be both stupid and cruel to ignore or to underestimate, even to undermine. For often, as Wordsworth said, we murder to dissect.'

Better. But was that really the truth either?

Jason Fletcher was still awake, though Sorrel, lying beside him, was not. If he put out a hand and laid it on her gently rising and

falling stomach, he would be able to feel beneath her skin a life
he and she together had made. When the child was born, they
would have been living in Tanbury, in the house he had coveted so
greatly in his teens, for many months; he would have been back
in the town, which his family had left many years ago, but where
the Jason Fletcher he himself now – and the world too – knew had
properly begun, a curiosity-ridden, eager, ambitious adolescent
with a feline face and a cheeky smile.

Why then did he feel so uneasy? The 'phone call from Kevin
Lalland had, no doubt, done much to disturb his equilibrium –
indeed who was better at doing that than Kevin? (Despite his own
words to the contrary, let him stay in Madrid!) – but, truth to tell,
he had been feeling disquietude all day. He was tired, of course;
getting things ready for the removal men who were coming early
in the morning was a back-aching business, and he had not wanted
Sorrel to do any heavy work. Maybe, he had said to himself, he
should have informed the Varney brothers about his having bought
'The Cedars'. It was not *Dan's* reaction he was afraid of – however
Dan felt, he would shear his emotion of its spikes in presenting
it to the outside world – but crazy James's. For that letter of yesterday had been crazy, hadn't it? At odd moments of the day he
had even felt upon his face what James had reminded him of –
outrage-strengthened fists pummelling him in the cricket pavilion,
after, quite fed up at last with his arrogant taunts and boasts about
his pedigree, he had told James just what his father had been.

The bedside light was still on – Sorrel always fell asleep long
before Jason could. His hand stretched out for a book. (He could
not know that at this very moment James himself was searching for
nocturnal reading, and was about to have his hopes of happiness
horribly destroyed.) An Evelyn Waugh novel – no, he didn't want
that! A pamphlet on discrimination against coloured people in the
armed forces – interesting, but hardly for the small hours. And the
manuscript of Hampton Varney's actually completed *magnum opus*:
Prospero, which, by means of diplomacy and subterfuge, he had got
hold of from old Father Lalland. Well, perhaps he would read a few
pages of this – to remind himself of the now fallen Varneys and the
former proprietor of the house he himself now owned.

He would return to Madrid. He wanted to see the city in conditions other than a planned day of Fascist riots. Faces – anonymous and amiable – swam into his inner vision like trout in a stream coming towards the bank to be fed: they were the faces of the Spaniards whom he *wanted* to know, who loved peace, who lingered over *bric-à-brac* in the Rastro and laughed over strong coffees and cold beers in bars, who played spirit-charged music from mountains their forefathers had intrepidly penetrated years before, who cast admiring eyes at numinous yet vigorous Goya murals, and did not flinch from confrontation of that painter's journeys into psychic darkness – knowing that at the end of these a new clarity could be found, illuminating so much of humdrum life that had hitherto seemed incomprehensible. Spaniards like that student encountered just now from Red Andalusia.

Besides Kevin's fondness for Madrid would mean that the two of them would visit it often.

Dan laid down his pen. The black case, he realised, which had engendered so many emotional happenings, was still standing untouched on the top of the humming, vulgar little fridge. Now he went up to it – with a reverence that neither James nor Kevin would have been ashamed of – and lifted up its lid. The harmonica, with James's name upon it, shone at him, the moon transformed into rectangular metal. Dan thought: I almost believe it could make music of its own accord, could conjure melody out of the light it seems to contain. And the time it would surely play for me would be 'Wildwood Flower'.

James stumbled out of the clump of Portugal laurels that had sheltered him through the measureless, wet, apologetic dawn. His pointless vigil was over now – brought to an end by a huge pantechnicon turning slowly, unwieldily, into the drive.

Drunk with weariness, James had almost forgotten why he had forsaken Father Lalland's roof for an uncomfortable watch over his old home. A home to which the light had brought no life! The windows had, in grim triumph, turned opaque with the emergence of the watery sun; behind the brick walls silence had continued palpably to preside. 'The Cedars', thought James, has become a gabled tomb for all the various hopes of the Varney family. And what need had there been for Father Lalland's airgun? From time to time he had fingered it, masturbating death. But in truth the only dangers that could advance towards him would do so through the exertions of his sad, strained memory.

The furniture van had drawn up now in front of the flight of steps that led up to the porch. On that porch he had so often played his harmonica, and people walking up the lane had stopped to listen to him. Well, all that would never happen again. And someone new, it appeared, was coming to live here.

Perhaps this new purchaser of 'The Cedars' was none other than his dear brother Dan himself! But no, James told himself sadly, that could not be: nothing so welcome could occur in his life now. The newcomer would be someone who could not recognise the dishevelled, gun-carrying man now lumbering from the shrubbery with the movements of a troubled animal.

At the idea of the astonishment, the alarm he must undoubtedly give rise to, James emitted a sudden, loud, wild laugh, for which his body did not seem quite responsible. Yes, he thought, spluttering now on the driveway, he really should offer himself to whoever-it-was as guardian of 'The Cedars'. After all, harmonica's bridegroom, deprived of his bride, was in want of a new identity.

THE END

Afterword

I wrote the greater part of *Harmonica's Bridegroom* in Spain in 1982, mostly in Madrid where I was living, but also in Ávila where I went for Holy Week. Though that wonderful old city is situated high up in the mountains, it was warm enough there to work outside. All the scenes of the Varney brothers at their Oxfordshire Grammar School and Dan's visit to Father Lalland at his vicarage I composed in the shade of Ávila's sturdy medieval walls, with storks on their nests above me. I had arrived in Madrid the previous autumn, shortly before the weekend with which the novel opens: that of pro-Fascist demonstrations to mark the sixth anniversary of General Franco's death. A young man sitting on a bench in the great Paseo de Recoletos, in much the same posture as the novel's Kevin, stayed in my mind and joined with a memory of another young man playing a harmonica in an Oxfordshire garden. . . . And so the novel came into being – how could I join up these two imaginatively compelling pictures? All my novels have begun as answers to this kind of question.

I was in Spain to do research for my study of Federico García Lorca, *Lorca: The Gay Imagination* (1985). This demonstrates, through close analyses of individual works, that Lorca's homosexuality, in both his inward and his outward life, was a prime mover for his writing, overtly so in productions not published in his lifetime: the strange surreal drama, *El Público* and the beautiful sequence *Sonetos del amor oscuro*. It was a fascinating time to be in Spain anyway, one that Lorca of all people would have appreciated – increasingly like watching a fairy-tale princess wake up to realise her own long suppressed potential and to recognise people from her past sent into exile by a merciless government.

Gay life acquired an almost luminous paradigmatic quality in those years. But I was myself very much preoccupied with the whole relationship between the public and the private faces of homosexuality. I came to Madrid with an Italian partner who witnessed the Franquistas that night with me, and who overturned and dominated my life for about six years. We have gone on to live in different countries, but still have irregular but very personal and enjoyable conversations over the telephone. So the novel written in Spain was bound to concentrate on gay relations and identity, even though its eponymous figure stands wholly apart from them, and, for all the emotions he elicits from the two central characters, gives no sign of understanding, let alone sympathising.

This is the point at which to say that, while nourished by personal concerns, *Harmonica's Bridegroom* isn't, in any usual sense of the word, autobiographical at all. No connections whatsoever with Fascism in my family (my father was professionally connected with a reconstructed Germany), and my younger brother is a successful publisher and writer and a loving husband and father. The problems in our lives, mine and his, were, on the surface anyhow, of a quite different origin from those of the people of the novel. But I still subscribe to T. S. Eliot's idea of the 'objective correlative'. The central situation or pattern in a novel or play must at once be interesting in its own right and informed by matter from the very depths of one's creative being. It should stand independently from oneself while constituting a living metaphor for one's existential predicament.

This metaphor will inevitably contain what the English poet and critic (and friend of mine), Stephen Spender, called one's own 'grammar of images'. It is these that struck me most as I reread *Harmonica's Bridegroom* for this new edition: badgers and the quiet of the woodland when these animals emerge from their setts in the evening (these occur again in my novel of 2012, *After Brock*); Bluegrass and Appalachian folk-music and the country-dance tunes of the British Isles; the importance to the waking life of dreams in which the familiar undergoes transformations. And same-sex communications. I felt apprehensive reading the book's erotic scenes again; earlier '80s writing was apt here to be over-insistent, and a well-known publishing house, which has taken my work since, turned this novel down because of them. But I found myself content with their emphasis on psychic as well as physical need, on what is best described in Gerard Manley Hopkins' great line ('God's Grandeur'): 'There lives the dearest freshness deep down things'.

An English bookseller friend of mine said to me: 'Do you realise that all that's life-enhancing in the novel takes place in England? Once you get to the English parts, especially those set in the countryside, the key alters.' I can't disagree. Madrid and Tennessee are crucibles through which my characters must pass, but they themselves are all entirely English with sensibilities formed (like my own) by English landscape and English mores. Being English is far from easy, and since Valancourt Books did me the honour of deciding to reissue *Harmonica's Bridegroom*, three public events have happened, all of them germane to my novel of 1984, to vindicate this statement.

The first was the death of Margaret Thatcher and the de facto state funeral accorded her. This dismayed me, and millions of others; our three-terms prime minister did more than any other single person to wreck the social body of England (Scotland and Wales rejected her decisively). I was actually in Spain for the blood-stained triumphalism of the Falklands War, watched its hideous events on Spanish TV in a café near my Madrid apartment. US readers may not appreciate the cruelty within the UK of Thatcher's abolition of the Greater London Council (carried out because its politics didn't consort with hers), leaving London the only large city in the world without its own administration. Or that of the Miners' Strike, the bitter protracted conflict belonging more to the earlier 19th century than the 20th. But those American readers who respond to the search for consummated love in my book will surely feel hostility to Thatcher's iniquitous Clause 28, brought in to prevent any 'promotion of homosexuality' in public-financed institutions, making schoolteachers and librarians uneasy, nervous. Happily the Conservative administration today has not only apologised for it but the Coalition which it leads has been responsible for Gay Marriage becoming a legal fact of British life. Unhappily the same government has given into pressure from the interests of the rich and landed and approved a cull of badgers (on the questionable grounds that they help carry bovine TB) in the face of huge public and parliamentary opposition and the scrupulous findings of a well-researched official scientific survey. In the designated regions it was intended that 70% of these mysterious, beautiful, largely gentle animals, who mean so much to the Varney brothers, should be shot; in the event, far fewer died, largely because of the vigilant presence of human protesters.

The people of my book were very much alive to me as I reread it. They are a lot older now. Neither James Varney nor Kevin Lalland have had easy lives, but after another breakdown set off by his firing his rifle at Jason Fletcher, James was redeemed by his practical side. He turned to breeding and rescuing dogs, and in the course of this work, fell in love with and married a young woman working for his kennels. They have a son, Luke, who, like his uncle Dan, trained as a doctor and is now a General Practitioner with a young family living in the same county, Oxfordshire, as his father. Kevin was diagnosed HIV positive in the earlier '90s, and, now back in England with his own textile design business, has thriven well on medication, and strikes everyone as a gently competent, reliable person. Perhaps he has turned against his former lifestyle a little too thoroughly; he is unshakably quietist in his beliefs and habits. Dan was more shattered by the events that the novel relates than he had imagined would be the case. When he was offered an academic-cum-hospital post dealing with speech and vocal disorders in Sydney, Australia (at a very good salary), he took it – and after a couple of years found an Italo-Australian partner, Raimondo, a hospital technician with whom he lives in a relationship that still maintains its warmth. He rarely returns to the UK now, however. By contrast Jason Fletcher (now on his third marriage) has his own TV arts programme, and a regular op. ed. newspaper column to boot. He lives in London – and, by an irony where this novel is concerned – has a house in El Escorial, near Madrid.

What writers was the author of *Harmonica's Bridegroom* most influenced by? Interestingly, in the light of my above remarks about Englishness, all of them seem to me to have been American: James Purdy, who was kind enough to praise my book in print (specifically commending the badger episodes); Eudora Welty (I was to be the Eudora Welty Professor of Southern Studies in Jackson, Mississippi for 1985-86, and wrote a full-length study of her for Virago Press); Walker Percy, particularly *The Last Gentleman* – and, when at his very good best, my friend the late Reynolds Price. If we remember that Purdy set much of his finest work in

West Virginia, state of Eudora's maternal family, then all these
writers can be thought of as Southerners. Maybe it was they, more
than any others, facing up to the cruelties within their own society
and opposing them with their own hard-earned humanitarianism,
who understood the English psyche most deeply, and I tried my
best to learn from them.

PAUL BINDING

Bishop's Castle, Shropshire

November 28, 2013

ALSO AVAILABLE FROM VALANCOURT BOOKS